Daughters of Eve and Other New Short Stories from Nigeria

Edited with an Introduction by Emma Dawson

Critical, Cultural and Communications Press
Nottingham
2010

Daughters if Eve and Other New Short Stories from Nigeria, edited by Emma Dawson.

World Englishes Literature (Fiction)
General Editor: Emma Dawson

The right of Emma Dawson to be identified as editor in this work have been asserted by her in accordance with the Copyright, Designs and Patents Act, 1988.

Introduction and other editorial material © Emma Dawson, 2010.

Individual stories © the contributors, 2010.

All unauthorized reproduction is hereby prohibited. This work is protected by law. It should not be duplicated or distributed, in whole or in part, in soft or hard copy, by any means whatsoever, without the prior and conditional permission of the Publisher, CCC Press.

First published in Great Britain by Critical, Cultural and Communications Press, Nottingham, 2010.

Cover design by Andrew Dawson.

All rights reserved.

ISBN 9781905510276

CONTENTS

Map of Nigeria

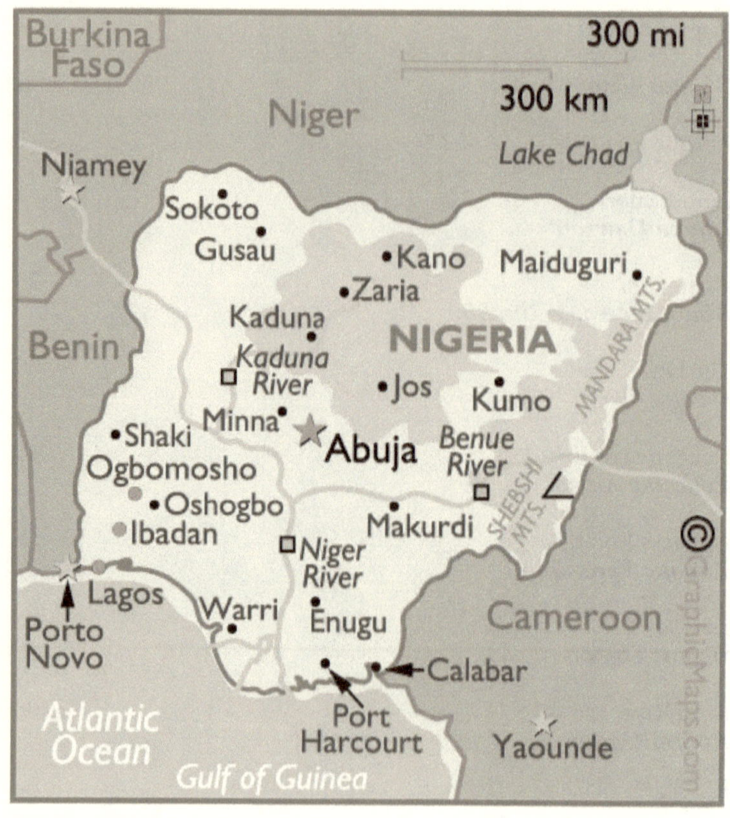

GENERAL EDITOR'S PREFACE

This volume belongs to the Fiction series of CCCP's World Englishes Literature imprint. This series focuses on the production of new writing in English, specifically new World Englishes fiction – a term which is defined in the introduction of each publication in the series. Country anthologies of new writing in English feature here, writing which is newly sourced, edited and presented with a critical introduction.

Each country anthology of new writing goes through a sequence of processes. Firstly, a call for short stories is launched electronically through email lists of writers, writing groups, universities and other relevant organisations. Once submissions have been received and read, a journey to the respective country is arranged by the editor in order to meet with the writers who have submitted their work as well as to offer an opportunity for others who have not yet heard of the project to come along and learn about it.

Making the journey to the country in question is paramount and this is what makes the CCCP's country anthologies different from other anthologies of new writing in English. The journey to meet the writers is one that is made in order 'to listen' and not 'to tell'. The World Englishes Literature imprint as a whole explores being beyond the postcolonial, by 'listening' to those who know, who are writing the literature *now*. This stance diverges markedly from anthologies compiled using already published (and recognised) literature, as well as anthologies which are compiled from 'the Western armchair'.

The critical introduction to the country anthologies benefits from this act of 'listening' and, in doing so, aims to present an accurate portrait of the writing emerging from the country in question. The visit to the country also affords the editor an opportunity to research the history of the place and culture, emerging criticism and contemporary literary events, all of which concern themselves with writing in English. All discussions with writers, readers, teachers and other interested parties who contribute to the debate on writing in English are audio-recorded in order for the material to be reproduced in a sensitive and accurate manner.

The final process is a re-opening of the call for submission within a limited timescale. This is conducted because very often, after the editor's visit to the country, writers continue to hear of the project and wish to submit their work. On the editor's return to the UK, the selection of entries is made in consultation with a second editor and reader. Selected writers are paid for their submissions.

The World Englishes Literature Fiction volumes are compilations of short stories which range from 3,000 to 10,000 words in length. The idea motivating such an anthology of short stories is to offer the reader an accessible and manageable 'taste' of a country's contemporary fiction writing in English. The short story also allows a country's writers to explore a variety of contemporary themes and concerns as well as exhibiting the linguistic diversity of the land in question.

Most of the writers presented in the country anthologies will not be 'known' to the Western reader and also possibly not even to many readers in their own countries. This is a basic aim of the series: to promote new, emerging writers, often unknown to the West, writers who have not been 'endorsed' by Western publishing houses, but whose writing tells wonderful new stories in wonderful new ways.

Emma Dawson

ACKNOWLEDGMENTS

How many modes of transport can you take to get to Lagos airport, Afam? Dump the pick-up, grab two (suspension-suspicious) *okadas* and then hail a taxi at the airport limits – that's how to get to the airport on time – just! Thank you, Afam, not only for getting me to my flight but also for your kindness during my time in Lagos. Thanks to your brother Chuma also, who suggested it in the first place!

Ladi and Dupe – thank you for your warmth and hospitality that came out of the sale of a piece of West African fabric! Wishing you all the best for your future plans.

To all those at 'The Cottage' in Lekki, I have warm memories of whiling away a rain-drenched afternoon in the lobby interviewing people about writing in English in Nigeria.

Thank you to all the writers who submitted in order to be considered for this anthology: keep writing, keep being who you are. A special thank you to the writers who feature here for working with me on editorial changes and considerations. I am honoured to have worked with you and to have produced *your* anthology.

E.D.

INTRODUCTION

This introduction will begin by defining the term 'World Englishes' and explain how this relates to 'World Englishes Literature'. It will go on to address the situation in Nigeria, offering a brief history of writing in English in the country and the specific context of Anglophone writing, as it is often called. It will cite the major contributors to this movement. The introduction will conclude by outlining the nature of the contributions to this anthology, the writers and the themes that are present in this contemporary collection of new writing.

1. Defining 'World Englishes Literature'

The term 'World Englishes Literature' is inextricably linked to a field of linguistic interest, 'World Englishes'. The term 'World Englishes' is used to encompass the notions of 'new Englishes' and 'New Englishes' (Jenkins 2006: 22-23). According to Jenkins (2006: 22) 'new Englishes' resulted from the first diaspora, and are to be found in the United States, Canada, Australia, New Zealand and South Africa. By contrast, 'New Englishes' (note the upper case 'New') resulted from the second diaspora, and is understood as being the product of situations in which English has been learned as a second language or is spoken as a language within a wider multilingual selection of languages: such scenarios would include, for example, Indian Englishes, Nigerian Englishes, Singaporean or Philippine Englishes. In short, not only is the linguistic production different of 'an English' and 'English as a Lingua Franca' (ELF), but the cultural, functional and ideological aspects are also at variance between the two.[1]

Jenkins' definition of 'New Englishes' and 'the second diaspora' (2006: 22-23) may have been influenced by the earlier work of Platt *et al.* (1984) who referred to the phenomenon as a 'New English' (note the singular). According to Platt *et al.* the four defining criteria for a 'New English' are as follows:

1. It has developed through an education system. This means that it has been taught as a subject and, in many cases, also used as a medium of instruction in regions where languages other than English were the main languages.
2. It has developed in an area where a native variety of English was *not* the language spoken by most of the population.
3. It is used for a range of functions *among* those who speak or write it in the region where it is used.
4. It has become 'localised' or 'nativised' by adopting some language features of its own, such as sounds, intonation patterns, sentence structures, words and expressions.

(Platt et al. 1984: 2-3; original emphasis)

Thus Jenkins' notion of 'new Englishes' and 'New Englishes' (which supersedes the work of Platt and colleagues) are included in the understanding of 'World Englishes' for the purposes of this introduction and the imprint of which it is part.

Kachru's (1982) model helps to highlight the extent of the meaning of 'World Englishes', as his model of the Englishes of the world demonstrates that the 'Inner circle' (although it does include the UK) constitutes the 'new Englishes' (that is, the result of the first diaspora, according to Jenkins) while the 'Outer circle' constitutes the 'New Englishes' (that of the second diaspora). Kachru's model also offers a third dimension to the global production of Englishes, namely that of the 'Expanding circle'. In summary, Kachru's model (of Inner, Outer and Expanding circles) can be taken as wholly representational of what is meant here as 'World Englishes' language production.

---

[1] See Tan *et al.* for further discussion on the difference between EFL and the Englishes of the 'Expanding circle' (specifically 2006: 84-94), as well as Kachru and Nelson for discussion on EFL *versus* ESL in an Asian context (2006: 25).

Kachru's (1982) model of the spread of English around the world remains one of several base models from which we understand the tripartite *linguistic* phenomenon that is 'World Englishes': the Inner, Outer and Expanding circles roughly correspond to the concepts of English as a native language (ENL), English as a second language (ESL) and English as a foreign language (EFL) respectively. The Inner circle includes the United States of America (USA), the United Kingdom (UK), Canada, Australia and New Zealand; the Outer circle includes nations such as India, Kenya, Malaysia and Singapore; and the Expanding circle includes nations such as China, Egypt, Israel and Japan (see Melchers and Shaw 2003, which devotes a detailed chapter to each of the three varieties).

Even in the Inner circle – that is, countries in which English is the native language – other languages may be spoken. In order to demonstrate how these languages are different from the dominant language, I will identify them as 'diaspora community languages' (see Kalra *et al.* 2005 for diverse discussion on notions of 'diaspora and hybridity'). In the United States, Spanish, Italian and Hebrew are spoken (and written) as diaspora community languages. In the United Kingdom, languages such as Hindi, Punjabi, Gujarati, Bengali, Urdu and Jamaican patois are spoken (and often also written). Numerous other languages of diaspora communities settled from first generation to third or fourth generation in Canada, Australia and New Zealand can also be similarly categorised. Moreover, any amalgamation of either a 'diaspora community language' or a language *per se* with the 'English' of an ENL country will therefore produce yet another 'English'. For example, in the UK, British Asian English is categorized by its own lexemes, phonology and grammar, but British Asian English shifts and changes, depending on whether the variety of British Asian English is spoken by people of Pakistani origin or, say, of Indian origin. Equally it differs (in regional accent, grammar and/or lexemes) depending on where in the country the variety is spoken.

In addition, within the 'Inner circle' there are languages which do not fit into the category of being one of Kachru's Inner circle's Englishes (American English, British English, etc.), or one of the 'diaspora community languages' (Hebrew, Punjabi etc.). The languages that do not fit into either of these two categories can be defined as being Indigenous languages, although this term can hold its own semantic problems. For the USA these languages are

(American) Indian languages, for the UK they are Scots, Welsh or Gaelic, and in the cases of Australia and New Zealand there are languages of Aboriginal origins. There are many Indigenous languages that I have not mentioned here and this is because I hope that this brief overview of the language situation(s) in the 'Inner circle' has illustrated sufficiently the complexities of Kachru's notion of 'Inner circle'.

In summary, we can see that Kachru's model is helpful in conceiving of the Englishes of the world and accommodates, to an extent, the complex situation of the multi-Englishes of the Inner circle. Can, therefore, this notion simply be transferred to the formation of 'literary' uses of World Englishes? My own answer to this question, perhaps curiously, is no. Indeed, I would wish to dismiss the 'Inner circle' notion, which is undeniably applicable to language use, as unhelpful in explicating World Englishes *literature*. When the *linguistic* voices (of World Englishes speakers) become *literary* voices (of World Englishes writers), it is my own view that, while Kachru's 'Outer' and 'Expanding' circles remain useful concepts for an explanation of what World Englishes literature is, this is not so of the 'Inner' circle: in my definition, that is, World Englishes literature is *never* produced from the Inner circle.

The issues at stake in this argument are not simple questions of geography, spatial proximity to the English 'Standard', or characteristic linguistic properties: it is more how these matters, in a certain combination, produce varied kinds of writing, some of which I would call World Englishes literature, and some of which I would not (although they are all in play). The lines of this debate have long been drawn up in historic theoretical arguments around colonialism and postcolonialism and the conceptual role played in these debates by the voice of the 'subaltern' (Spivak 1988).[2] Likewise, there is often an assumption that writing from the Outer or Expanding circles is always to be explained by the nature of the

---

[2] 'Postcolonialism' or 'postcolonial studies' is understood to span many disciplines (history, cultural studies, ethnography), but for our purposes the term refers to its deployment within literary studies. The term will also be used without the (often deployed) hyphen. Boehmer (2005: 3) distinguishes between 'postcolonial' as being pre-Second World War and 'post-colonial' as being post-war. I shall not deal with 'post(-)colonial' notions of literature to the extent that differentiations of such nicety will be required.

'gravitational pull' of the language of the Inner circle. But in my view the multiple features which determine the voice of a World Englishes writer are not defined by the notion of the voice being that of the 'subaltern' – whether geographic, linguistic, cultural, ideological, or all of the foregoing. World Englishes writers are less and less interested in their putative subalternity to a former colonial power and more and more interested in what constitutes, positively, the identity of the culture from within which they write. Similarly, they are less and less likely to worry as to the relation of the English they use to the notionally 'original' English of the Inner circle. I might therefore best encapsulate my definition as follows: *most (but not all) World Englishes literature explores the culture(s) of the country and people from which it is written (these countries belong to Kachru's Outer and Expanding circles); usually the literature employs the English of that place (to a lesser or greater degree); and, moreover, the writer chooses to write in that English over other languages in which she could alternatively write.*

It follows that World Englishes literature is not a synonym for postcolonial literature, although many countries with a history of (for example) British colonialism produce World Englishes literature. The voice of World Englishes literature is not one that necessarily laments postcoloniality or one that wishes for the 'subaltern to speak' (Spivak: 1988). Rather, World Englishes is (as it were) post- postcolonial, and although its writers may remember and even celebrate a defining moment of political independence from a colonising power (as in India in 1947, Nigeria in 1960, Kenya in 1963, or the Philippines in 1946), it also includes a generation of writers who do not.

In short, this anthology, and the imprint of which it is a part, invites readers to move beyond the appreciation of Anglophone writers in relation to their colonial past (which is, predominantly, the inflection which has been given to discussion of their work). It does so in the belief that there are many other avenues for discussion and appreciation of this enormous body of writing. I shall suggest some of these alternatives in the further discussion which follows.

2. World Englishes Literature in Nigeria

World Englishes literature production in Nigeria has been well founded, explored and canonised over the past 50 years. It is framed with the names of Achebe and Soyinka and Nigeria remains one of the most prolific and ever-growing World Englishes literature nations globally. And yet, Nigeria has struggled and continues to struggle with a sense of a 'national literature'. In a polyglot society and one moreover divided geographically into distinct groups – in particular the 'Hausa' Muslim North and the 'Christian' Igbo/Yoruba South - Nigeria is not an easy place to talk of in terms of a neatly defined sense of national literature. Achebe himself recognises the difficulties of the Nigerian language situation in *Things Fall Apart*:

When they had all gathered, the white man began to speak to them. He spoke through an interpreter who was an Ibo man, though his dialect was different and harsh to the ears of Mbanta. Many people laughed at his dialect and the way he used words strangely. Instead of saying 'myself' he always said 'my buttocks'. But he was a man of commanding presence and the clansmen listened to him. He said he was one of them, as they could see from his colour and his language. The other four black men were also his brothers, although one of them did not speak Ibo. 'Your buttocks understand our language,' said someone light-heartedly and the crowd laughed. (1986: 104)

The history of Nigeria explains to a large degree why a sense of 'nation' is problematic. Originally, 'Nigeria' was three colonial territories. 'Nigeria' *per se* was comprised of 'The North', 'The South' and 'Lagos'. Each territory was administered independently and by 1945 the north (The Hausa), the southeast (Igbo) and the southwest (Yoruba) had their own capitals as well as budgetary and council infrastructures in place. Soyinka (1996) dedicates much discussion to a sense of nation in his book *The Open Sore of A Continent*, in particular in relation to 'ethnicity' or 'tribe' and a sense of 'location' or 'geography' (19-30). Soyinka suggests that if a 'nation' is not indeed the physical, the geographical or the tribal, but rather the 'will' of the people, then Nigeria should be considered as a 'non-nation'. In an elegy to Chinua Achebe at the age of seventy,

Soyinka (2002) writes of 'their nation':

> Ah, Chinua, are you grapevine wired?
> It sings: our nation is not dead, not clinically,
> Yet. Now this may come as a surprise to you,
> It was to me. I thought the form I spied
> Beneath the frosted glass of a fifty-carat catafalque
> Was the face of our own dear land – 'own', 'dear',
> Voluntary patriotese, you'll note – we try to please.
> An anthem's sentiment upholds the myth. (68)

But how much of this notion of 'nationhood' is necessary for a sense of a national literature? Surely what Nigeria does possess is a vehicle that is ostensibly not Hausa, Igbo or Yoruba. Rather it is 'Nigerian' in that it is heard nationwide across all the 'ethnic' labels: Nigerian English. It is of course not that simple, not that uncomplicated or easy. Nigerian English has occupied a difficult position and continues to challenge a sense of 'literary' status in a society that is prolifically publishing Anglophone writing year after year. Fifty years ago, however, Achebe would write a 'Nigerian' novel in which we witness him code-switch between English, Igbo and Nigerian English (or 'pidgin', as it has often been described). In the late 1980s Achebe wrote: 'As long as Nigeria wishes to exist as a nation it has no choice in the foreseeable future but to hold its more than two hundred component nationalities together through an alien language, English' (Ashcroft *et al.* 2006: 268). The content of this anthology will focus somewhat on Achebe's choice of the adjective 'alien' and suggest that what we read *today* is not an 'alien' English but rather a Nigerian English, a familiar and rooted English which gives a sense of 'Nigerianness' today.

It is essential to look at the evolution of Anglophone writing over the past fifty years in Nigeria in order fully to appreciate what today's emerging writers are actually engaging with. In Achebe's novel *Things Fall Apart* (1958) there are many incidences of the use of Igbo, which is always italicised. Such uses are demonstrated through terms of address, greetings and interjections:

'*Nna ayi,*' he said.
Aru oyim de de dei! flew around the dark, closed hut [...]. 1986: 64)

All these instances of Igbo are made accessible to the English reader by paraphrase or by their inclusion in the glossary:

In fact, the medicine itself was called *agadi-nwayi*, or old woman. (1986: 9)

[...] because their dreaded *agadi-nwayi* would never fight what the Ibo call *a fight of blame*. (1986:9)

The elders, or *ndichie*, met to hear a report on Okonkwo's mission. (1986: 9)

And in the nine villages of Umuofia a town-crier with his *ogene* asked every man to be present tomorrow morning. (1986: 7)

ogene: a musical instrument; a type of gong. (1986: 152)

By contrast there are fewer examples of Nigerian English (or pidgin) in the novel:

'Yes, sah,' the messenger said, saluting. (1986: 149)

Today, as this anthology should prove, the balance in terms of code-switching is otherwise. More occurrences of Nigerian English appear, interspersed with other Nigerian languages at times. Whether this manifestation of Nigerian English is symbolic in any way of a shift in the notion of the Nigerian nation is impossible to say, and is indeed outside the scope of this anthology, but what remains central is that the identity of writers in Nigeria, writing in English, has shifted and continues to shift to what this anthology claims to showcase, writing which is beyond the post-colonial.

In 1966, Povey wrote, 'the last decade has seen the beginning of a literature in West Africa' (258). He quotes the founders of this new literature as being Chinua Achebe, Cyprian Ekwensi and Onuora Nzekwu, measured, he says, 'if only by the professionalism of their productivity' (259). He goes on also to venerate Soyinka and his first novel, *The Interpreters* a book which, for Povey, 'may stand as a goal for other novelists' (260). This celebratory view of emerging writing was not, however, shared by all. Nkosi also writing in 1966, argued:

[…] the reader who declines to delude himself must admit that he is bored by the endless parade of heroes caught between the old order and the new, of young lovers divided by tribal barriers which they are unable to breach however large their nobility and fierce their passion, by the Utopian novels of the independence struggle, and the equally simplistic tales of a post-independence world gone sour. One longs not so much for new themes as for fresh treatment – for a wider breadth of vision and an originality of language to match it. (7)

Nkosi was writing over forty years ago, and we are left wondering if Nigerian writing today is doing what Nkosi asks for, if we can say today that Nigeria writes 'beyond', employs 'fresh treatment', with a 'wider breadth of vision and an originality of language to match it'. Nkosi's 1966 paper closes with this: 'Soon, I hope, enough younger writers will emerge to shake even more profoundly the present Establishment. The talented among the Establishment will not worry' (11). Ken Saro-Wiwa was certainly one of those writers who emerged to shake the 'Establishment'. His *Sozaboy* (1985), a political satire on the Nigerian Civil War, is a seminal text in the evolution of Nigerian writing in English. This text marks a move towards what Nkosi (1966) talked of as 'a wider breadth of vision and an originality of language to match it' (7). The language employed in *Sozaboy* was described by Saro-Wiwa himself as being 'rotten English' – a mixture of Nigerian Pidgin English, broken English and occasional flashes of good, even idiomatic English (1996: Author's Note). The story explores life on the Ogoni during the Civil War, in particular the experiences of 'Sozaboy', the traumas and suffering he endures.

The period between Achebe's *Things Fall Apart* and Saro-Wiwa's *Sozaboy* is roughly equivalent in length to the period from *Sozaboy* to the present, and once again we see a corresponding change in Nigerian writing in English. There are factors, I would like to suggest, that have impacted Nigeria's writing in English very recently, in the last five to ten years, which make way for Nigerian writers *comfortably* to express themselves linguistically (and indeed thematically) in ways that previously have not been so easy or so prevalent. Nigeria is one of a few World Englishes literature producers enjoying this special position. It has certainly helped to nurture new writing that it could occur in a garden of Achebe,

Soyinka and Saro-Wiwa. From the works and prizes of the author Chimamanda Ngozi Adichie writing in English in Nigeria has gained greater confidence to be what it is currently. It is regrettable, however, that it was the West which endorsed the excellence of Adichie's novel *Purple Hibiscus* before her own nation got the chance to celebrate it. Adichie certainly upholds the Nigerian tradition of excellence in Anglophone writing, but as she spends more and more time away from Nigeria, what comes into question is how 'Nigerian' her writing will remain. Her recently published collection of short stories, *The Thing Around Your Neck* (2009), has all the already well-visited Adichie motifs of university life, riots, imprisonment - but it is the powerful motif of migration and diaspora that frame this particular collection of stories. The stories 'Imitation', 'The Thing Around Your Neck', 'On Monday Of Last Week', 'The Shivering' and 'The Arrangers of Marriage' all deal with migration or diasporic living, and this is a clear shift away from her two novels that deal so much with 'Nigeria'. Questions of diasporic Nigeria and Nigeria *per se* continue to present themselves, but are far from always being similar. Western publishing houses have, of course, influenced this development as they have, predictably, looked to publish Nigerian writing which is largely diasporic, such as that of Ben Okri.

Povey wrote in 1967, 'Although publication of most fiction continues to be undertaken in London, there is some evidence of the beginnings of local publication, largely of the ephemeral writing' (417). Povey does not clarify his use of 'ephemeral' but his review does offer us for consideration a point in history at which Nigerian publishing of Anglophone works started to take shape. There is and always has been a key factor in publishing in Nigeria – commercial viability. Unfortunately Nigeria still suffers from making Nigeria's emerging writers' works affordable. In an interview with *Wasafiri*, 'New writing and Nigeria', Adichie (2006: 56) comments: 'before you can afford to buy books to read for pleasure you need to have disposable income, which is something in decline in Nigeria'. Omole (1991), also argues that, despite the availability of texts increasing on account of affordable prices, the 'art' of Anglophone writing is not accessible to everyone, and suggests:

Indeed, only people who are very competent in the English language or initiated into their verbal artistry can understand their private metaphors, imagery, symbolism, idioms, and strange diction. As a corollary, they seem not to be too concerned with the significance and impact of their art on the masses of their society. Such works are invariably inscrutable to the generality of their potential readership, that is in a second language situation. […] Their works still largely address problems in their society, but apparently not for the appreciation of the entire community, save those who can decode their texts. (598-599)

Notwithstanding Omole's scepticism, publishing in Nigeria is growing and affordable books are definitely more numerous with the emergence of publishing houses such as Cassava Republic (see **http://cassavarepublic.biz**) and Kachifo Limited (see **http:// www.kachifo.com**). These publishing houses are committed to the dissemination of emerging World Englishes literature from Nigeria and have recently published Adaobi Tricia Nwaubani's *I Do Not Come To You By Chance* and *To Saint Patrick* by Eghosa Imasuen. Further emerging writers also feature on these publishers' websites through interviews, blogs and discussions. Such writers include Tolu Ogunlesi (who is featured in this anthology), Jude Dibia and Lola Shoneyin, to name a few. The future for Nigerian World Englishes literature is very bright, but it remains important that Nigeria fosters its own 'home-grown' writing talent, endorsing it *in* Nigeria, and venerating it in being *from* Nigeria.

3. Write There, Write Now

This collection of short stories explores universal as well as local issues – stories of love, of profound hurt and damage as well the haunting, the scary, the serious and the profound all feature here.

From simply accepting a 'caller unknown' call on his mobile phone, Santi finds himself on death row. This scenario in Abubaker Adam Ibrahim's 'Night Calls' starts a chilling account of one man facing the death penalty, having been cruelly set up by a gang of criminals. But there is hope. Aided by one of the prison warders, Santi discovers a chance to save his life.

'The Discovery' is an eerie tale. Having lost their close friend a matter of days before in a nasty accident in a car workshop, Emeka finds his friend Amaechi on the side of the highway with his mini-van, broken down. The rain pours and they jump into Emeka's car to let it pass, and they fall asleep, only to be woken by strange noises and the sound of a creaking tree. They run from their car to watch wide-eyed from the other side of the road. They return to find that the tree has fallen exactly where they were sitting and that Amaechi's mini-van is on blocks. What then happens changes lives forever.

Peter Ike Amadi takes the reader to the 'other' side of Lagos in his short story of crime, gangs and underworld. In 'Daughters of Eve', Caesar works for *Scoop* magazine, and the rooting-around for his next story takes him to places he's never been, to encounters with the Buchos brothers he would rather not have, and deep into the murky world of human trafficking.

Her visits to a troubled academic are always conducted in the dark. Out of curiosity and personal desire, she goes to visit him to see if the rumours are true. Has he gone mad since his return from prison? Why doesn't he leave the house? Will he ever turn on the lights? Moreover, will *she* ever ask *him* if the lights can be turned on? 'Lightless Room' by Jumoke Verissimo explores the unspoken and the unseen.

Mr Ignatius Imodibo is no ordinary man. *Payday* is no ordinary CD. Today is no ordinary day. It starts when Mr Imodibo goes for his bath in his *face-me-I-face-you* accommodation. He takes *Payday* to the firm as promised, has his mobile stolen, passes a few hours locked up in prison only to find himself back at the firm happier and richer than first thing in the morning. Ifeanyi Ogboh's clever tale of entrepreneurship is rightly entitled 'Payday'.

Rotimi Ogunjobi's story 'Road Rage' tells of Musa and his ageing red Mercedes making the morning journey to work through Lagos traffic. Between them they put the world to rights and chat with, argue and speculate about many of the passing vehicles and their drivers.

'Fragile', a haunting tale of the reunion of two childhood classmates in unexpected circumstances by Uchechukwu Peter Umezurike, tells a difficult narrative about the injustices of time and the many things we are unable to forget.

Saying 'No' to her husband is not an option. In Tolu Ogunlesi's 'No Woman Left Behind', Modinat struggles to convince her husband to use a condom. Modinat meets Mama Titi at the doctor's and she is only too happy to help Modinat with her 'issue'. But does Modiant succeed in convincing her husband or does she push him so far that their marriage is put into jeopardy?

Nostalgia is at the heart of Soji Cole's 'My Little Stream'. The protagonist journeys back home to Nigeria after some years in the USA. Although he is able to recognise the primary school he went to, amongst other things, the eponymous stream is less easy to locate.

Alpha Emeka's story, 'Haunted House', is true to its title, a family saga that sees a daughter travel home on her father's request to celebrate his sixtieth birthday, only to find that her father has taken Kate, one of her former classmates, as his wife. Kate has a dubious past and the daughter's memories of Kate's time at college are all bad. But the time back in Nigeria reveals links between people that turn things far worse than anyone could have ever imagined.

In 'Guitar Boy', by Emmanuel Iduma, the protagonist Higo finds Mofe the most beautiful of the waitresses in a restaurant, but it is Candida he thinks about all the time, not Mofe. He goes to visit Candida at her house, imagining that he will finally have the opportunity to tell her how he feels, but he discovers something terrible on his arrival and his life changes forever.

What this brief overview of contemporary Anglophone literature from Nigeria offers is the opportunity to see that we are at a crucial juncture in its evolution. The new writing presented here demonstrates in various ways the changing voices, styles, genres and positions available to the Anglophone Nigerian writer today. This anthology is intended as a marker in its history.

References

Achebe, C. (1986). *Things Fall Apart*. Oxford: Heinemann.

Adichie, C. N. (2009). *The Thing Around Your Neck*. London: Fourth Estate.

Adichie, C.N. (2006). 'New writing and Nigeria' *Wasafiri* 21:1.

Adichie, C. N. (2005). *Purple Hibiscus*. London: Harper Perennial.

Ashcroft, B., G. Griffiths and H. Tiffin (2006). *The Post-colonial Studies Reader*. London: Routledge.

Boehmer, E. (2005). *Colonial and Postcolonial Literature*. Oxford: Oxford University Press.

Imasuen, E. (2008). *To Saint Patrick*. Lagos: Farafina.

Jenkins, J. (2006). *World Englishes*. London: Routledge.

Kachru, Braj B. (1982). *The Other Tongue: English Across Cultures.* Urbana: University of Illinois Press.

Kachru, Y. and C. L. Nelson (2006). *World Englishes In Asian Contexts.* Hong Kong: Hong Kong University Press.

Kalra, V. S., R. Kaur and J. Hutnyk. (2005). *Diaspora and Hybridity.* London: SAGE.

Melchers, G. and P. Shaw. (2003). *World Englishes.* London: Arnold.

Nkosi, L. (1966). 'Where does African writing go from here?' *Africa Report* 11:9.

Nwaubani, A. T. (2009). *I Do Not Come to You by Chance.* London: Weidenfeld and Nicolson.

Omole, K. (1991). 'Linguistic experimentation in African literature'. *Literary Review* 34:4.

Platt, J., H. Weber and M. L. Ho (1984). *The New Englishes.* London: Routledge and Kegan Paul.

Povey, J. F. (1967). 'African literature in English'. *Books Abroad* 41:4.

Povey, J. (1966). 'Contemporary west African writing in English'. *World Literature Today* 63:2.

Saro-Wiwa, K. (1985). *Sozaboy.* Port Harcourt: Saros International.

Soyinka, W. (2002). *Samarkand and Other Markets I Have Known.* London: Methuen.

Soyinka, W. (1996). *The Open Sore of A Continent.* Oxford: Oxford University Press.

Spivak, G. (1988). 'Can the Subaltern Speak', in C. Nelson and L. Grossberg (eds.), *Marxism and the Interpretation of Culture.* London: Macmillan.

Tan, P. K. W., V. B. Y. Ooi and A. K. L. Chiang (2006). 'World Englishes or English as a Lingua Franca? A view from the perspectives of Non-Anglo Englishes', in R. Rubdy and M. Saraceni (eds.), *English In The World.* London: Continuum.

Night Calls
Abubaker Adam Ibrahim

The worst thing about being on death row is the waiting, the nightmares, the interminable introspection and the verdicts you pass on yourself. In the darkness, in the night, the verdict; whether guilty or not, keeps coming back, the incident - the one moment of madness that will haunt you till your dying moments, when you dangle from the noose like a piece of meat in an abattoir. That was Santi's ordeal as he sat on the cold floor in the damp, overcrowded cell, his mind still refusing to believe that he was just a number waiting to be scrubbed off the board.

He had been reading that night, that first night, when the call came. He picked up the phone. It was a new number.

'Hello,' he said huskily.

'Hello,' it was female. She spoke with a honeyed voice.

'Yes?' he did not recognize the voice.

'Hello, who is this?' she asked.

He felt offended. 'Excuse me, you called my number. I should be asking you that.'

'I want to speak to Sylvia.'

'Ah, I think you've got the wrong number.'

'No, this is definitely her number,' she was insistent. She sounded sure.

'I don't think so. This has been my number for close to a year now. Perhaps you should check the number again.'

'Well, okay.' She terminated the call.

She had a wonderful voice, he thought, as he put down the handset. She reminded him of the little birds twittering at dawn on the palm tree. He resumed his study, squeezing his eyes to readjust and focus on the tiny print. Then the phone chimed again. In the night, it sounded loud, like an angry bell tolling. It was her again.

'Hello,' he said.

'Hey, I think you are right,' she said, 'I got the wrong number.'

'Oh!' he chuckled, 'Okay.'

'I forgot to apologise for waking you up. I know it's quite late.'

'Well, no problem. It's all right.'

'I did wake you up, didn't I?'

'No, I was just eh... doing something.'

'Something? Like what?'

He wanted to tell her it was none of her business but he thought better of it.

'I am reading.'

'So, you are a student then?'

'Yes, and you?'

'Same here. Computer Science.'

'That's great. That's what I am studying too.'

'Where?'

'Jos. What about you?'

'Zaria, A.B.U.'

'That's... terrific. So, what's your name?'

'Farida. What's yours?'

'Santi, they call me Santi.'

That was how it started. They talked about their studies, comparing notes. Then they got personal. Every night, a little past midnight, she would call him and they would talk for hours about the rains, about the future, about randy lecturers, and then they started talking about love. That was how he fell in love with the honeyed voice at the other end of the line. They exchanged pictures through MMS. Her beauty, he thought, matched her voice. She was slender like the fresh stalk of budding bean and had a smile that, for some strange reason, reminded him of a clear spring running gently over white rocks. His feelings for her grew.

Two months later, she invited him to Zaria, so they could meet face-to-face. He had been looking forward to seeing her, so, he went, on a weekend, when the sun rose with a smile, as if blessing the union forged over the GSM interface. He got to Zaria and took an *okada*. She guided him on the phone to the threshold of her heart, her home. She was waiting for him at the door when he arrived and he realised that she was even more beautiful than in the picture. He kept thinking about that clear spring each time she smiled. She asked him in, served him food and soft drink and sat by him. They were overwhelmed and just kept looking at each other, smiling, sighing contently, happy to abide in the fragrant presence of a promising love.

'See what GSM has brought me,' she said and they both laughed. Then they relaxed and started talking, excited like teenagers after their first kiss, hidden away in an empty classroom. Her grace charmed him and he watched her every move, every gesture, with eyes veiled with adoration. She grew, in his mind, from the myth on the phone to a living goddess – his Aphrodite. She magically took his breath away and he was willing to surrender his life then, in the fatuous manner of lovers, so that nothing else could wipe away the memory of that sight of her enchanted splendour.

Then she excused herself and went to the bedroom. He stood up, looking at her framed photographs on the walls, on the mantelpiece beside the vase of synthetic flowers. He began to wonder if she lived alone when he heard her scream. He raced to the bedroom, calling her name, his heart thumping wildly. He rushed in and was caught by a blow behind the head. He fell face down and saw that he was lying next to the gaping face of a man, frozen horridly in death. He drew back and was struck again. There were two other men in the room, hefty like prized wrestlers. Farida was behind them. She watched as they trounced him, his screams filling only his own head, before he lost consciousness.

He woke up on a damp floor that gave off the offensive smell of stinking shoes. He was cuffed and shackled and his left eye was almost blinded. He was conscious of what he believed were his bloated internal organs and he thought all the bones in his body weighed twice as much. He was in a police station. A policeman came and had him straddled on a chair. He said he wanted to take a statement. Santi explained what he could remember and the policemen started laughing. The officer in charge nodded to one of them and they brought out a prepared statement and asked him to sign it. They would not let him read it, they just wanted his signature. When he refused, they had him beaten and tortured. He eventually signed the statement.

Weeks later, when he was arraigned in court for the murder of Farida's husband, he still could not believe it. The First Information Report said he went to see the deceased and they started arguing about money. Farida's husband, the FIR said, went into the bedroom to get some money and that was when Santi followed him and stabbed him fourteen times. Farida screamed and passers by came and apprehended him in the act.

Santi could not prove that he signed the statement under duress and the police had three eye witnesses – Farida and the two giants. And so, after months of attending a trial that seemed designed to convict him, he was found guilty and sentenced to death. He was thrown into prison, awaiting the hangman with as much anxiety as he had awaited his fated meeting with Farida.

Somehow, he developed a relationship with one of the warders, an elderly one who had the courtesy to listen to his story. In Santi, the warder saw himself when he was young. Listening to the convict's tale, he thought they were even more similar than he imagined; the naïveté, the lure of a promise of love, youthful fantasies: utopia. He sighed and shook his head. Sometimes, he would smuggle bread, *garri*, soap, salt, at times even pepper, for Santi to make the intolerable meals have the semblance or taste of something edible.

*

She surprised him again when she paid him a visit. He thought she would be remorseful but she smiled with the hint of triumph when she saw him in his ill-fitting death row uniform, as if she had won a bet. The only thing he could think of saying to her was: 'Why, Farida?'

She shrugged. 'They have not been treating you well here,' she said. 'That's not right. They should treat you well. See how wretched you are looking, God!'

'Why did you do this to me?' he asked, looking deep into her eyes.

She laughed this time. A demon stirred in him, urging him to wring her throat and, at least, die for having actually killed someone.

'I don't know,' she said at last. 'Maybe I shouldn't have done that to you. You are such a handsome guy. We could have had a thing together, you and I. We would have made a wonderful couple.'

He gaped at her, startled by her impunity, her heartlessness. He still could not believe she could do such a thing; that innocent smile, those tender eyes, that voice – the sound of happiness itself.

'I should kill you,' he said through his teeth.

She looked deep into his eyes and shook her head. 'You can't do it, Santi,' she said. 'You don't have the eyes of a killer.' She gave him the fruits and some items she had brought for him. He looked at the bag and tipped it over the edge of the table. The things scattered on the patchy floor.

'Just get lost, okay!' he shouted. 'Just go, enjoy yourself while I take the fall for you. What pains me is that I could have done it for you, for love. I could have taken the fall for you, on my own terms. I am that stupid, you know. But you just had to set me up, you bitch! God!'

She was shocked. The anguish in his voice, the sincerity got to her. Perhaps for the first time, she felt a tinge of remorse. She stood up with tears in her eyes. 'Santi,' she sighed, 'I have been most unfair to you. Perhaps, I should explain to you why. You deserve to know that, at least. I will tell you next visiting day, I promise.' She turned and left. He was taken back to his cell, seething, hating himself.

Eventually, he told the aging warder about Farida's visit. He told him what she said. The old man with a clearer head was the first to see the opportunity.

'We could get you out of this,' he said, excited. 'If we could get her confession on tape, it would give you some leverage. You could walk out of this.' So, he smuggled in a cheap recorder with new batteries and a tape. He kept them for Santi until the next visiting day. They tried it out, it worked. The problem was that the buttons snapped with such a loud *kpak* that would give them away. So Santi had to start recording before he was really close to her. The idea gave Santi a new breath of life and he looked forward to that day with the candle of hope burning brightly in his heart. The day came. They had the tape hidden on Santi. They waited and waited. The hours crawled until the day went by. She did not come. Santi took it to heart. He developed a fever and hoped to die. He adamantly refused to get well.

Unexpectedly, she came. They rushed through concealing the recorder under his clothes, having made sure it still worked. Weakened, he trudged to the visiting room and there she was, in her angelic splendour. She brought him food and some other things. She had to bribe her way in, she explained.

'So, you are back,' he said. 'Why the hell are you back? What do you want with me?'

'I heard you were sick. I knew this condition they are holding you in will certainly kill you,' she said. 'How can anyone live like this? It's inhumane. Anyway, I have been thinking about you. I missed our night calls, our… conversations. You won't believe how much they mean to me, those conversations.'

'See where they got me, those… conversations.' He was sarcastic.

'I know how you feel. The truth is… I am actually in love with you.' Her voice quavered. He looked into her eyes, startled. She was close to tears. 'I have been missing you but I know you will not believe me,' she said.

'That hardly explains anything, does it?'

She dabbed her eyes. She was actually crying. 'What is killing me is that you will never believe me.' She went on explaining how she was missing him, how she could not sleep at night because she was thinking about him, about their night calls. She cried so much he wanted to hug her but he feared if he had the chance to, he would end up strangling her. But all that rambling would not help him. He would soon run out of tape if she kept going on like that.

'Explain it to me, Farida, because I don't understand,' he said. 'If you love me, why would you do such a thing to me?'

She took her time dabbing her eyes. 'I will tell you my story, as I promised. I will tell you why I did what I did.' She told him about her marriage to her husband. How he had bought his way to her parents' heart, how they had forced her to marry him, how she hated the man's guts and how she had planned, for long, to free herself with the help of her boyfriend. It was this boyfriend, she said, having learnt of her relationship with Santi, that planned the frame up and executed it. She told him how he had threatened her life if she did not cooperate and how he had promised to kill her mother if she refused to marry him. She told him how she, too, was a prisoner, like him, how she too was waiting for her own hangman.

'I don't think you will see me again,' she said at last. 'But I just thought you deserved to know the truth, and to know that I truly love you.' She rose to leave. 'I will pray for you, Santi, everyday, until I die.'

The old warder was waiting. Anxiously, he seized the recorder. 'Did you get it? Did she confess?'

Santi nodded.

The warder played back the tape. The recording was scrappy and statics frothed from the device but the voices could be heard. 'Ah, so she loves you, eh?' he smiled and fast forwarded the tape. He pushed the play button and listened. 'Yeah, yeah, more love talks.' Again he hit fast forward, then play. 'This girl really has it in for you,'

'Just a little forward, now,' Santi said.

The warder forwarded the tape and pushed the play button.

'...I will tell you my story, as I promised...' Farida's voice was saying.

'That's it,' Santi shouted, excited.

'... I will tell you why I did what I did. You see, my husband was a rich man but I did not want to marry him because I had this... boyfriend I really liked. He was...' there was a brief silence, then the device snapped to a stop. That was where the recording ended.

THE DISCOVERY
Ikeogu Oke

Yours was an unusual car. 'The type that'd never embarrass its owner in public,' you'd often said. Nor was it demanding.

Not a battery drainer like Kaodiri's jeep. Not a fuel guzzler like Amaechi's minivan. Those friends of yours had known nothing but torture from those vehicles of theirs.

Your spine stiffens with cold each time you remember Kaodiri's last encounter with his jeep. It was at Okechi's mechanic workshop. Kaodiri had asked you to come with him so he could check what was wrong with his battery.

'It doesn't retain charge,' he'd said.

'Maybe the alternator,' you'd suggested.

You'd gone with him hoping that, after days of refusal, he'd agree to come with you for a bibulous evening so you could discuss his recent quarrel with Nkiru, his fiancée.

Nkiru, looking emaciated, had visited you early in the morning, the previous Monday, and asked you to intercede with Kaodiri.

'Please beg him for me. It was my fault. Beg him for me, please,' she'd pleaded.

She wouldn't give details of her wrongdoing despite your prodding, and Kaodiri hadn't betrayed any sign of animus towards her.

'Don't you think you're overreacting?' you'd asked, with a slight quiver to your voice.

'Maybe he is,' she'd replied, tamely.

'So what's he probably overreacting to?' you'd prodded her once more.

She said she was ashamed to say what it was but assured you she didn't cheat on him.

'It's ju-ju-ju just that,' she'd seemed on the verge of blurting out what it was (with a stammer), when the tears started streaming down her cheeks, choking her. 'Ask him to forgive me, please. Ask him to give me one last chance,' she'd managed to say, sobbing, as you walked her to the gate.

*

It happened before your very eyes. Kaodiri was standing behind Okechi who was standing on a low stool, stooped over the engine of his jeep. Okechi had a bowl of petrol in his left hand with which he was cleaning the battery head with an iron brush in his right hand. Suddenly sparks flew off the battery head and ignited the petrol. Instantly he swivelled, his eyes filled with horror at the prospect of his having to drop the bowl of burning petrol on the engine, or of the petrol fire melting the plastic bowl in his hand; he needed to act in a split second, and in the ensuing desperation he threw the burning petrol on Kaodiri's face. In a moment Kaodiri's cry of anguish pierced your soul as you dashed off to safety uncomprehendingly. And when you turned back you saw him, his hands clawing at his face as he rolled in a nearby puddle, in a frantic effort to put out the fire that was consuming him.

When you, Okechi and a group of sympathizers arrived with him at City Hospital thirty minutes later, there was no dark spot left from the skin of his face down to his shoulders. His eyelids were burnt so badly that his eyeballs showed. On his cheeks a fatty fluid ran from red vertical wounds that stood out where his hands had been clawing to extinguish the fire. A mixture of blood and lymph dribbled down his neck to the mattress in the Emergency Ward, which soon filled with the smell of his burnt-out hair, and the blisters on his torso peeled off with every irresistible effort to turn his pain-wracked body.

You only needed to see the look on the doctors' faces to bow your head in despair. When you raised your head and looked around you noticed that Okechi had disappeared; and soon after you and Kaodiri's people had seen his body wheeled into the morgue the next morning the news filtered in that Okechi had been found dead in his room, his corpse clutching an empty bottle of barbiturates in its right fist, and that it had taken some struggle to prise the bottle off its lifeless grasp.

When you visited Nkiru the next Friday, on the eve of Kaodiri's burial, she was dressed in black, her shrunken face still mysteriously beautiful as you'd always thought it to be. You had gone to apologise to her for having seemed to let her down, as if Kaodiri might have evaded that ghastly fate if you had succeeded in delivering her message, in reconciling him with her. But you had both remained speechless throughout the meeting, your eyes fixed on the ground, your mind playing back the horror of Kaodiri's death and of your close shave with that bowl of burning petrol. Barely a week after you left you received news of her having suffered a mental breakdown.

*

That was two days before your next meeting with Amaechi.

'What's going on?' you'd asked him, having cleared your car off the highway.

'It's at it again,' he'd replied, his voice shrill with frustration as he drew back and squinted at you from his squatting position beside one of the rear tyres of his grounded minivan, his palms browned with dirt and grease stains.

'Take it easy,' you'd said gently, consolingly.

'Take what easy?' he'd snapped, his tone laced with bile.

The tyre, when you looked closely, was flat, broken in places in fact, with the tube spilt out like intestines after a disembowelment.

'What happened?'

'I just heard '*Kpuuwaai*' and managed to control the thing. I then came out and this was what I saw,' he'd said as he stood up and gestured towards the broken tyre. 'For thirty minutes I've been trying to bring out the stupid thing and change it with the spare, so I can continue my journey, but it has refused to budge.' Amaechi sighed raspingly after he'd said this and then raised his right hand so you could see the blood dripping from a cut he had received from a loose wire sticking out of the broken tyre. 'To think this monster has just swallowed all my pay for the month. And this is all it has to show for gratitude.'

'And where did that come from?' you'd asked half-audibly, pointing at a slightly bent nail stuck to the broken tyre.

'I hadn't seen that! It must have picked it before the explosion. This is one vehicle that will pick anything with its tyres just to leave you stranded in such middle of nowhere.' You almost thought the vehicle had a will of its own the way he said that, and with a sweeping gesture whose scope took in all the surrounding landscape.

'Take it easy,' you'd said once more as you returned from your car with First Aid.

*

No sooner had you stopped the bleeding than the sky turned stormy. Suddenly the rain was pelting down so heavily that you both had to scurry into the front seats of your car for shelter, almost drenched, leaving Amaechi's jack, wheel spanner and your First Aid box beside the broken tyre.

Nor could you tell when you dropped off to sleep.

When you awoke and whispered Amaechi's name in the freezing chill that stirred about, you could only hear the sound of his slow and tired breathing. The night was braced in a cold and ghostly silence, then a pale half-moon seemed to peep at you from behind overarching dark clouds and cast a sombre light on the surrounding bushes whose effect, combined with the hooting of a distant owl, was to intensify your feeling of dread.

'Amaechi,' you'd whispered again.

For a while he remained all silence and tired breathing; then you noticed sluggish movements as his slow, shadowy body seemed to rise in the middle of a trance.

'Amaeechii,' you'd whispered once more, stretching some of the vowels as if to hint at the fear that had begun to tug at your heartstrings.

'Won't you allow me to sleep?' He'd drawled out the reply, turned on his side, and curled up, foetal.

'What sleep?' You'd barely voiced the question, wondering if you'd have to shake him, when a tree in the nearby bush tumbled down with a creaking sound and landed across the bonnet of your car with its huge trunk, its wet leaves covering a shattered windscreen.

'What's this?' He'd drawled out again as he started suddenly and ran with you into the cold night.

From the other lane of the highway you saw people gather round your vehicles and the fallen tree. You could see the cluster of their *mpanaka* lamps and the sooty smoke rising from the naked yellowish flames fluttering in the night breeze. You could see the light haze that ringed their wicks like halos, shimmering in the distance. Unmistakably, the men wore singlets and loincloths and the women had wrappers tied round their chests.

After a while you had managed to cross the highway to see what had become of your car.

Having taken in the scene, aided by the smoky but bright lamps, you realised how close the tree had come to crashing into the front seats where you had sat with Amaechi. The bonnet was a flattened wreck. The front tyres had taken a violent wrench from the impact of the fallen tree and were now shaped like legs beneath knocked-in knees. Your skin suddenly filled with goose bumps as you gazed at the front seats, and you felt a cold thrill as if a drop of ether had just landed on the tip of your spine. When you told those villagers that you had been in those front seats as the tree fell, the men impulsively flung their mouths open and the women clasped their chests with their arms.

'Your god is awake,' one of the men broke the ensuing silence, having seemingly overcome his disbelief.

'Truly, their god is awake,' echoed one of the women, her voice shaking vicariously. Then you noticed that she was looking at your groin and, once your eyes caught hers, she looked away. And then you realised that there had been wetness where she had fixed her gaze, and that it was still warm; you felt an overwhelming need to prevent others from discovering that embarrassing secret you seemed to share with her alone, more so as she had sneaked out on realising that you had found out. Then you suddenly reached for a searchlight from your pigeonhole and contrived a diversionary march towards Amaechi's minivan.

'What's this?' It was Amaechi's horrified voice as you pointed the searchlight on the minivan and you both realised that it was now standing on stacks of broken blocks.

You'd quickly opened the door on the driver's side and pointed the searchlight at the dashboard. The slot for the car radio was now an empty hole. And when you turned back in the direction of your car you saw empty spaces where the villagers had been standing. Then you noticed movements in the nearby bush as if some men were trying to free their legs from the entanglement of creepers. All you could sense afterwards was some strange rumblings in your bowels and your knees seeming to buckle as you fled to the other lane of the highway.

*

'What's going on?' you had wondered aloud as you arched up your torso from a hospital bed.

'Gently,' it was Nneka's anxious voice as she eased you back to a reclining position.

As you were later told, a man had found you stretched supinely by the highway. He said he could only risk bringing you to the hospital because you bore some resemblance to one of his classmates in secondary school.

'I wouldn't have done this for all the wealth in the world and risk police suspicion as the culprit, with all the trouble that could come with that, especially if he doesn't recover to reveal what really happened,' he'd said as he left you in the charge of the hospital staff with the necessary provisions.

You had realised that you could not say what really happened though it had to do with your desperate moves to escape whoever was hiding in the bush that night. You had realised, too, that whatever transpired on the highway that Friday night had meant that you and Amaechi couldn't be at the Father Tansi Cathedral the next day to attend your younger sister's wedding and that you couldn't bear the thought of having to make an excuse, however genuine, to justify your absence to her.

Your x-ray revealed internal bleeding and fractures, which could explain the pains that made your nerves squirm intermittently, but not also their own origin. Were you knocked down by some hit-and-run driver as you dashed across the highway? Did your pursuers finally catch up with you in what might have seemed an endless flight for your life and, having mugged you to their fill, left you for dead? Had the terror and injuries of that night left you amnesiac? The puzzle would remain unsolved when you remembered to ask of Amaechi and was told that the police had yet to locate him since that night.

'Some men of the black cloth have repeatedly gone to his mother every morning to ask for *mobilisation* since she reported his disappearance at their station near Mkpor bridgehead.'

'*Mobilisation* for what?'

'To fuel their search vehicle.'

'And she gives them?'

'What choice has she? Her only child. They also keep returning by noon to ask her for *contribution*.'

'And what's that for?'

'To *fuel* their stomachs. They keep telling her that they can't find a missing person on an empty stomach if she hesitates to *cooperate*.'

'How do you know?'

'She came here and told me. She's been here everyday since you were admitted. She just left before you came to.'

'Such men of the black cloth. Even poor widows.' You'd said that with all the disgust you could muster as you ended the conversation with Nneka.

*

Then it dawned on you that a week could be too long not to have found anyone apparently ambushed at night by a wilderness of a highway and pursued to God-only-seems-to-know-where.

Try as you did, you could not shake off the thought that you might have seen Amaechi for the last time that night, that as you made to obey the instinct to flee on sighting those crouching shadows you might have been parting with him for good. Then came those tears that stung your eyes before rolling down your temples to wet the pillow that propped up your head, tears of a heart-corroding grief made more poignant by its seeming lack of justification, and more devastating, for it might never find relief in a proper burial for the friend to whose sudden disappearance it traced its origin.

*

Your grief deepened with your recollection of your last tiff with Nneka. It was your third year in a childless marriage and your mother had suddenly started dropping unsavoury hints about 'Nneka's behaviour' so often that they had become difficult to ignore.

'I know you'll say it's because I wanted you to marry Amaeze and not her. That doesn't stop you from trying to find out. Don't our people say that whoever is being helped should also help himself?' she'd said the last time she raised the issue, sounding half-persuasive and half-cryptic. And she had seemed quite right as you mumbled the neatly printed quatrains on the card you later fished out of a remote corner of Nneka's wardrobe:

The Sleep I Lose…
(To Nneka)

The sleep I lose would not matter,
If one day should lead me to your heart;
And you will find nothing on earth to barter
With the place I'll give you from the start:

A place full of beautiful things like your eyes,
And your lips whose colour is that of a ripe rose,
And your skin whose hue is that of the sunrise,
And the good blunt tip of your African nose.

With love,
E. O.

'What's this? Who gave this to you?' you'd fumed, shaking the lines at Nneka as she came in from the parlour, your fist clenched, your eyes reddening and bulging out, your face taut with a grimace.

'What?' She'd wondered aloud as she took the card from you, looking confused. 'It's the poem you gave me ten years ago. Aren't E. O. your initials? Emeka Obi!'

Your mortification was palpable as she waved the card at you. It had struck you afterwards that she had never called you by your full name, that she had always called you Emeka, just Emeka, and with an unmistakable undertone of fondness, and then you wondered if you had not asked for it, for her having to call you by your full name this once, her lungs filled with bitterness and disgust.

'Now I can see the special and incomparable place you promised me in your poem. I can see it in your incipient suspicion and maltreatment. I can see it in this unwarranted and distressful snoopiness of yours. I can see it, Emeka Obi. Can't you?' Her fruity voice rose to a bitter climax with the question, her eyes glazed with tears as she bit her lips in tense silence, looking fixedly at you.

'I'm sorry,' you'd said bashfully as you took back the card and withdrew to a corner to read the quatrains more closely.

'So why are you still keeping this?' You'd asked after a long silence.

'Because it was the reason I fell in love with you and agreed to marry you. Those lines…'

'Not the gifts that came afterwards?' You'd cut in gently, irresistibly.

'I can't remember what gifts.'

'The clothes? Shoes? Jewellery?'

'No! And I wonder that you haven't written me any other poem since then.'

You had left her presence wondering if she had sensed the truth behind those lines, behind your silence to her wondering that you hadn't *written* her any other poem. And then it struck you that you were far more indebted to Amaechi than you had ever thought. For when she wouldn't give you audience after several visits to her family house at Emene Hill, you had confided in Amaechi, telling him how smitten you were by her, and how unapproachable she had seemed.

Amaechi had listened with his eyes closed.

'I think I can help you out,' he'd said afterwards as he suddenly opened his eyes with a glare, his tone conveying both modesty and self-assurance.

But his subsequent refusal to explain how he could intervene to change your fortune with Nneka only deepened your craving to know, turning the withheld information from a tantalising morsel into an object of a desperate hunger whose distress gnawed at your bowels and quickened your heartbeat.

He rather asked you to see him in the evening of the next day, and you had left his presence with a tinge of frustration to your feeling of enthusiasm.

Your heart fluttered with anticipation as you knocked on the door and he opened and offered you a seat. The musky scent from your cambric bull shirt mingled with the lavender fragrance of the air freshener stuck on the far wall between two framed portraits at whose lower margins were inscribed 'Christopher Okigbo' and 'W. B. Yeats'.

You were seeing the portraits for the first time, but not the quartz clock that hung above them, creating an isosceles effect, whose white second hand glided silently across the face of the sea-blue dial notched with black markings. Not the well arrayed books that formed an inverted meniscus on the mahogany shelf. Not the granite carving of the *Ikenga*, the Igbo right-hand totem of goodwill, placed midway atop the shelf. Not the reading lamp borne aloft by the statuette of a black mermaid, placed at the upper left edge of the mahogany reading table, on the arabesque tablecloth, beside the ever-rising pile of manuscripts. Not the carved mahogany chair in front of the table, with its plush leather seat, feline legs and curved armrests. Not the canary in its metallic pink cage suspended from the white roof clear off the chandeliered ceiling fan. Not the small mattress with its quilted cover placed on the floor by the edge of the mimic Persian rug. Not the two gold fish in the mini-aquarium hitched to the far wall painted sky-blue like the rest. Not the centre table with its tinted glass top on a brass support. Not the empty ceramic ashtray on the centre table shaped like a hollowed-out turtle shell. Not the clipper-shaped enamel vase, which Amaechi's description two years ago as his 'ship of flowers' still lingered in your mind, placed next to the ashtray. And of course not the two chairs, replicas of the one in front of the reading table, in which you were now sitting with him.

'The portraits are nice in the ebony frames,' you'd said warmly, wondering how long you might have to wait before he would unveil his secret help with no further prompting from you.

'Our people say that the evening is not the right time to indulge in lengthy talk.' He said that just as you were about to inquire regarding the identity of the two men in the portraits, and then pulled out a sealed envelope from under the tablecloth.

'Take. Go and give it to her. Then simply turn back and go home. Don't open it.' He'd said as he handed you the envelope with the air of a medicine man prescribing and infallible charm.

A few hours later you had run back to him with the news of how Nneka had waltzed into your room soon after you delivered the envelope and grabbed you and smothered you with kisses. And you would wonder that he should simply gaze at you, even after you confessed that it was your first kiss and that it had been so satisfying that you could hardly care if you were never kissed again.

'Good for you,' he had managed to say as you made to leave his presence, his face looking mysteriously calm.

'What did you put in the envelope?' you'd asked.

'Maybe you'll find out someday,' he'd said, chuckling.

DAUGHTERS OF EVE
Peter Ike Amadi

> Quippe minuti
> Simper et infirmi est animi exguique voluptas ultio.
> Continuo sic collige, quod vindicta
> Nemo magis gaudet quam femina.
>
> Indeed it is always a paltry, feeble, tiny mind that takes pleasure in
> revenge.
> You can deduce it without further evidence than this,
> no one delights more in vengeance than a woman.
> - Juvenal, A.D. c.60- c.130

Undisclosed location, 3:45am, August 15, 2008

The room is swamped in darkness, the only illumination coming from a lone candle that flickers bravely in the corner but can do nothing to dispel the hot, inky blackness that came soon after dusk.

I sit alone, my only companions are my thoughts which are never pleasant companions at all but I have no choice because they are the only companions I will ever have.

My eyes watched the dripping candle unblinkingly, my body still and unmoving. I sit naked in bed, sweat streaming down my black skin in rivulets, soaking the sheets thoroughly.

Yet, I feel nothing. If not for my heart that beats like a wooden clock inside me, I might not even be alive but my spirit is long dead.

I guess I did die a long time ago, violently as I remember all too well, lying in the murky swamp in a spreading pool of my own blood while staring in disbelief at the star-filled sky.

I had been stabbed, stabbed and stabbed relentlessly by those I had considered dearest to me, the deepest cut had come from my other half, the one I loved more than anything else in the world.

It was she that had killed my spirit, the blade she held had severed the umbilical cord between my soul and my body, sending my spirit hurtling off towards space. Now it is just my body that is alive. I am nothing more than a zombie, a ghost of my former self, a demon that will feel nothing but hate, my path a wide straight road to Hell.

Revenge had been sweet; I had taken their lives one by one, tasting their horror and disbelief as I slew them without pity.

She had been the last and the sweetest. I made her beg for mercy as I tore her apart, limb by limb. I made her look into my eyes as I slaughtered her, savouring her screams of agony like fine wine.

But my thirst is not relinquished. There is still one more person I have to track down, one more soul I have to destroy before I am truly satisfied. Until his blood drips from my slavering jaws I will know no respite from the hate that eats away at me like cancer.

Edwin 'Caesar' Clark, we have a score to settle. I will not rest until I have your beating heart in my hands

Scoop Magazine Head Office, Adeola Odeku, Victoria Island, Lagos, 5:30pm, August 16, 2008

'My goodness, Caesar,' exclaimed Temitayo Oluwale, the editor in chief of *Scoop* Magazine as he rifled through the file of documents and photos in his hands, 'Where did you get this stuff?'

Temi was a dapper young man who loved wine, women and good food. He was also happily married. Bulky and vertically challenged, he reminded Caesar of a terrier. He had got to his present position by being very tenacious and ambitious. Caesar loved to hang out with him anytime they weren't working although he didn't approve of his philandering. Temi had a nice homely wife which Caesar secretly fancied. Kemi was big and cuddly and seemed to have some affection for him also. She thought nothing of giving him big hugs which he shamelessly enjoyed due to her generous bosom. Temi knew they liked each other. Caesar could tell from the lecherous sneer on his face anytime his wife entered his arms.

'You wouldn't want to know,' replied the young reporter. He was staring impassively out of the huge windows of the *Scoop* editor's office at the gridlocked Lagos traffic below.

Caesar wasn't going to tell him that he had dressed up as a woman to buy information off an informant in the organization. The stuffed pink, lace bra was still in his closet. He had no idea why he hadn't thrown it away. One day it would get him into trouble.

'If we print this it will start one hell of a storm.'

'That's the idea. What's the matter? Don't you want to print it?'

'I don't see why we can't. You've brought us all the possible facts and figures concerning this human trafficking racket. And I'm certainly not in love with Senator Kuti.'

'Neither am I. Once this hits the stands it will end his political career like a bullet to the head.'

'That's probably what you're going to get if you insist in this story going to press. Do you have any idea who you are messing with?'

'I'm not scared of him.'

'You should be. Do you know how many political assassinations have been linked to this guy? He's a mass murderer and he is sitting in the senate house in Abuja making policy with other lawmakers.'

'Well, they are probably all mass murderers themselves. After all you can't get involved in politics in this country unless you're ready to get your hands dirty.'

Temi looked at Caesar strangely.

'Edwin?'

'Yeah?'

'What about…? You know… her?'

'You mean my mom, the honourable Minister of Aviation, who happens to be sleeping with Senator Kuti?'

'Caesar…'

'It will be a pleasure to shoot down Mummy Dearest's lover. It will give me great pleasure indeed.'

'But don't you realize that could scandalize her as well? She's your mother for Pete's sake!'

'I wasn't the one who told her to sleep with the senator. She gets what's coming to her.'

'Damn it, Caesar!'

'Look, skip it!' he snarled, his voice like a fall of gravel, 'That's personal, alright? The relationship between me and my mom is my business. Are we clear?'

'Okay, okay, we're clear.'

'Good. I'll be off then.'

Caesar picked up his briefcase and headed for the door.

'Edwin?'

'What?' He impatiently placed his hand on the doorknob.

'This story isn't going to have a happy ending.'

'I know.'

Nkechi's Bar, Surulere, Lagos, 6:30pm, August 16, 2008

The Bucho Brothers were indeed an interesting pair. They could not be more different from each other. The elder brother was short and squat with a small bean head, while the younger one was tall, wiry and with a massive skull. Their only shared genetic trait was their ugliness which they had in spades. They both looked like deranged baboons that had recently engineered a prison break from the local zoo.

Another thing they shared in common was their depravity. They were bloodthirsty and lacked any form of empathy whatsoever. They killed people not just because of the financial reward but also because they greatly enjoyed their work. Their patented modus operandi was rape, torture and kill or sometimes just the opposite: kill, torture and rape. It didn't matter whether the victims were male, female or mongrel.

Clients who hired their services weren't just interested in sending their enemies to the great beyond with a mere bullet to the cranium. They wanted their foes to suffer horribly before being finally dispatched.

Suleiman, an aide to Senator Kuti, found them in Nkechi's Bar which was infamous for being a *rendez-vous* for killers and their contractors. Cops never bothered anyone in the bar. After all, Nkechi, the big boisterous Igbo woman who owned the place, was married to a police officer.

The Bucho Brothers didn't drink nor smoke and listened to Suleiman while sipping morosely from bottles of orange soda which irked the aide, as he was himself a chain smoker and a walking, breathing distillery.

'There's a lot of money in this,' Suleiman said urgently, 'We want her found and once you've gotten the item, take care of her in your usual style. Make sure nothing links my employer to the job.'

'Is The Boss aware?' Eddie Bucho asked. He was the elder one and arguably the smarter, if not sicker, of the two.

'Never mind that,' the aide said irritably, 'You should know that no contract is carried out without The Boss's stamp of approval.'

'Okay, just making sure.'

'Now find her.'

Caesar's Apartment, Lekki Phase 1, 7:00pm

I am good with a pick lock and before you can say 'Cheese!' I am inside his apartment. All the lights in the apartment are on, so I don't bother with the flashlight I brought.

His apartment is exquisitely furnished with state of the art electronic equipment and designer home décor. A surge of jealously courses through my veins, nearly incapacitating me. The idea of killing him appealed even more to me.

I walked into the bedroom, my mind going through various scenarios. I wanted him to die very horribly, even worse than my better half that betrayed me. My favourite weapons are knives. I decided I would use them again. Maybe I could tie him to the bedposts, tear off his clothes and stab him mercilessly. The fantasy aroused me.

I moved into the kitchen and noticed it was very clean but disused. A bachelor like Caesar probably never had time to cook for himself. All the utensils were there but looked more for decoration than actual usage. Maybe he deserved a last meal. I could cook his liver and feed it to him. His heart however I would have for myself

I was pleasantly surprised to see that he also had a set of knives, quite similar to the set I once owned and which is now in the hands of the police. How ironic!

I went into the living room and stood idly around, thinking. As usual, I was being too careful. That had always been my problem. I would check, recheck and double-check. I was never satisfied that my plans would go according to the letter. After all, if my partner in crime hadn't screwed up, Caesar would be dead and wouldn't have lived to tell everyone about me. That's why if you want things done, you have to do them yourself. Caesar had got wind of our operation and had nearly got me arrested. Meanwhile my partner was now cooling off in jail awaiting trial.

I decided I would not take any chances. I would hide behind the sofa and, as soon as he was inside, I would take him. Caesar had an uncanny ability of sensing danger. That's how he had escaped me twice before. But I had a good feeling about this. Caesar could not possibly outwit me this time.

I went into the kitchen, picked up the biggest knife from the set and went back into the living room. I chose a nice, big sofa and sat down to wait. My heart thumped with anticipation.

En route to Lekki Phase 1, 7:05pm

Oblivious to the noose of revenge tightening around his neck, Caesar did some shopping. He took a drive to the Palms Shopping Mall in Lekki and popped into Shoprite.

He bought some tubers of yam, a bag of rice and some seasoning. Caesar couldn't cook to save his life; he only bought them to impress female shoppers.

He had a hot-looking Itsekiri girl who did the cooking and cleaning in his apartment. Mary was well built with a killer body like most girls from Delta State. She liked to wear very scanty clothes whenever she was around and she was very a hardworking girl. Caesar admired the way her body glistened with sweat anytime she was busy and could spend all day staring at her and imagining stuff. He hadn't touched her yet and hoped he never would. That was the whole point. A little sexual tension was good for the soul.

He packed his groceries into the boot and gunned for home pushing his Benz through the remorseless traffic. Soon, his left foot was feeling numb by pressing on the clutch and Caesar swore he would switch to an automatic vehicle. The problem was that he thought automatic cars were for women and lazy men and that was why he felt British cars were superior to their American counterparts. He loved the feel of manual cars, especially the continuous wrestling with the gear stick. However, right there and then, he would have given anything to drive an automatic.

His phone was buzzing and he picked it up.

'Hello?'

'Edwin?'

Caesar stiffened and a frown creased his face.

'Hi, Mom.'

'Why are you doing this?'

'What?'

'Don't be smart with me! Why are you doing all this to discredit me?'

'It's not you I'm trying to discredit! It's Senator Kuti I'm after.'

'Why won't you stop harassing him? How many years have you been a thorn in his flesh? For six years now you've been accusing him of nonsense.'

'Well, I have evidence to back it up now. Senator Kuti is going down.'

'Not caring how this affects me, right?'

'You chose to sleep with him, Mom, maybe you should choose your sleeping partners more carefully.'

'You bastard!' she hissed. Caesar thought venom splashed on his face. He had no doubt that, had he been speaking to her in person, she would have slapped him.

'I'm not a bastard, I have a father, even if you chose to forget him.'

'I never forgot your father. Is this what it is all about? Using Senator Kuti to get to me?'

'This isn't about you or Dad, it's about doing the right thing. I am fed up with you people in government thinking you can get away with anything just because you're in power. Someone has to stand up to what is right and bring people like Senator Kuti down.'

'Do you have any idea how dangerous he is? He could kill you!'

'I'm not scared of him. If he does kill me, I'll love to know how that's going to weigh on your conscience. Maybe you can tell Dad how his only son was murdered by your boyfriend. Goodbye, Mother.'

'Edwin, wait...'

Caesar cut her off and tossed the phone on the passenger seat. He took a deep breath and fought the desperate sadness that welled up inside of him. He stared at the sea of cars in front of him, his face blank. He then looked at his hands and noticed they were shaking.

Lekki Phase 1, 7:10pm

Caesar was nearly home when his phone started burring again.

'Mom, just leave me be!' he began hotly.

'Hello?' asked a nervous female voice, 'Is that Edwin Clark?'

'Yes, this is Edwin speaking,' he answered, his eyebrow going up a notch, 'Who's on the line please?'

'My name is Debola. I need to see you immediately.'

From her voice Caesar placed her within her late thirties.

'Sorry, Debola but that's not possible right now. I'm about to go up my driveway. Now if we can reschedule...'

'I have what you want!' she cried desperately.

'Sorry?'

'I have information about Senator Kuti that will destroy him forever!'

Caesar was immediately interested but he smelled a trap.

'I already have enough to bring him down,' he retorted.

'Trust me, you have never seen anything like what I have. Meet me at the Plaza Hotel, Victoria Island, room 303. And please hurry. He's sent his dogs after me.'

'Debola...' The line went dead.

Caesar sighed and stared at the lights of his apartment.

Was this caller genuine? It wasn't the first time he had walked into such a trap.

But he knew, deep down, that even if it was a trap, he would still like to go, if only out of sheer curiosity.

He checked to see that his Browning 9mm automatic pistol was safely tucked in the glove compartment and made a U-turn.

Plaza Hotel, Victoria Island, 8:05pm

Caesar tentatively rapped his fingers on the door of room 303, his other hand holding the butt of his automatic which he hid under his sweatshirt. His senses were on high alert.

'Who's that?' rasped a voice.

'Debola, it's me, Caesar. Open the door.'

The door opened and Caesar tensed. A fair-complexioned woman of about thirty-seven years of age peered out at him. She was very tall and slim with an excellent figure, even though her face was rather plain. She was completely bald which Caesar found oddly erotic. If she hadn't looked so harassed, Caesar might even have found her attractive but, right then, she was clearly unsettled. She was wearing a see through blouse over a tight pair of jeans and Caesar had to try and ignore the fact that she wasn't wearing a bra.

'Please, come in.'

Caesar walked past her into the room which he noted had no other occupant. The door to the bathroom was open and that was also empty.

'You have something for me?' he asked as he turned to face her.

'Please sit down. Do you want something to drink?'

'Yeah, let me have some whisky with plenty of ice.'

Debola poured him a drink while Caesar watched her closely and handed him the glass. She also poured herself one and proceeded to gulp it down dry. Caesar smiled to himself. It was a Nigerian thing – if you offered someone a drink, you tasted it first to make it clear that you were not trying to poison your guest.

She sat down facing him and, after a moment's pause, began to talk.

'I used to work for Senator Kuti. I recruit local girls to be sent abroad for prostitution.'

Caesar leaned forward eagerly. My word, this is very interesting, he thought.

'I get paid very well for my services' she continued, 'This is important, so that girls who didn't know any better would want to be like me. I also convince poor families to give up their young ones, so they can go abroad to work as servants.'

Caesar winced. That was a job description he didn't fancy at all.

'Then I manage to convince young pregnant women to abort their babies and carry drugs in their wombs instead.'

'Oh, my God!' Caesar gasped in disbelief.

'I know,' Debola said sadly, 'I've done so many evil things for money. I have had a change of heart because I can't stand the dreams I keep having. It was when I witnessed my girls being raped and killed by my boss that I decided all this horror must stop.'

'You mean this man raped and killed more than once? Who is he?'

'Senator Kuti.' Caesar took in a deep breath.

'Can you prove it?'

Without a word she stood up and went to a pretty leather bag in the closet. She came back and handed him a photo.

Trying to stay calm, Caesar studied the shot. He nearly dropped it as if it had burned his fingers.

It was a picture of a young lady who was strapped naked on to a bed, her mouth gagged. A grotesque figure had mounted her and was pumping away. There was a look of satanic glee on his face and his features were unmistakable – it was the honourable senator alright.

A despicable image entered his mind and wouldn't go away: his mother's face replaced that of the girl. A hot blast of fury washed over him.

'How did you get this?' he asked quietly.

'I placed a hidden camera on timer when I saw that he would continue to commit these atrocities. Most of these girls didn't even make it abroad. He did them in his private apartment in Abuja. Most of the time, I was the one who picked up these girls.'

'Do you have copies?'

'No, that's the only one.'

'Then I have to get this to my editor friend right away. He's working on a story on the senator right now. Anything else?'

'No.'

Caesar stood up.

'Thanks for what you have given me,' he said, 'I'll make sure he doesn't hurt anyone anymore. His reign of terror is over.'

'There is something you should know,' she said quietly, 'It may seem unlikely but Senator Kuti isn't the one at the top of the food chain.'

'Really? Then who is?'

'There is a mysterious figure known only as The Boss. Whoever this person is masterminded the entire operation and Senator Kuti is just one of the many pawns.'

Caesar shrugged his shoulders.

'I'll love to find out who he is. Meantime I'll settle for the senator.'

He turned to go then turned back to face her.

'You must be in grave danger' he said softly.

'Yes, I am.'

'Come with me and we'll find a safe place to lay low.'

She smiled sadly and Caesar was suddenly depressed.

'There is nowhere for me to run, Edwin. Just make sure that the truth is exposed about the senator. Promise me that.'

'I promise.'

She came to him and kissed him softly on the lips.

'Goodbye, Caesar.'

'Goodbye, Debola.'

As Caesar drove away from the hotel, he couldn't stop thinking about her and the horrible things she had done. Would she ever find redemption? Caesar hoped so. This was a cold, cold world that forced normally decent people to commit sin. Things were never black and white, especially in Africa.

He picked up his phone and called Temitope.

'What do you want, Caesar? Don't you realize that I'm very busy? I am still battling with all this junk you gave me.'

'Well you'd better get the champagne glasses out while you're at it.'

'Why?'

'Because, Temi, I've got a pretty little picture that will look very good in that tabloid rag of yours.'

'Really? What's in it?'

'Just you wait and see. I'm on my way to your place right now. I hope your couch is free?'

'Should be unless you want to share the bedroom with my wife?'

'That's more like it. I'll just stay the night, then I think I'll leave own. Once this hits the stands, I'll need to lie low a while. Any ideas?'

'How about the town we were posted to as National Youth

Service Corps? That small town called Roni in Jigawa State?'

'Good idea. See you in fifteen minutes.'

At a particularly tight corner, he had to slow down to allow a smooth looking Honda Accord to cut past his Benz. He glanced indifferently at the two men in the front and wondered why God had created two people of such staggering ugliness. They stared coldly back and Caesar felt a chill crawl up his spine. Nasty buggers, he thought, and narcissistically glanced at his own reflection in the rearview mirror to safeguard his faith in God. With the road clear, he then sped off with the Benz giving a reassuring roar.

Benny Bucho was still staring at the receding car in the passenger side mirror.

'Did you see how pretty that guy was?' he asked almost wistfully.

Eddie grunted.

'Probably a fag.'

'Did you see the way he looked at us? He thought we were really hideous.'

'Well, we are not exactly visions of loveliness now, are we, Benny?'

'But that doesn't give him the right to look us like we were lepers!' Benny voice rose as his temper soared.

'Its okay, Benny,' Eddie said softly, 'Our looks don't matter. We more than make up for it in passion, right?'

'Yeah. Pretty punk bastard thinks he's all that but probably can't get it up. If I run into him in a dark alley I'm going to ass bang him till the fool nosebleeds. Then I'll snap his neck.'

There was a terse silence in the car as they drove into the premises of Plaza Hotel.

'You know what, Benny? The bitch is all yours. I'll just sit and watch. Once we've got the photo, you can have all the fun.'

'Watching is fun too,' remarked Benny and they both laughed.

Eddie was happy that his brother was smiling again. He knew Benny had been close to tears and, right since when they were kids, he could kill anyone who tried to make his kid brother cry. Now for some action.

Caesar's apartment, Lekki, 8:15pm

I was getting impatient. Where the hell was Caesar? I stood up and began to pace his living room. When I got bored with that, I prowled round his apartment. Eventually I ended up lying on his bed. I took off my clothes and began to pleasure myself imaging different ways I would cut him up.

I also thought about Mel the Butcherette, the racist psychopath that had nearly killed him in England. I was envious of her skill and intelligence but I was determined to emulate her. Caesar might have escaped her, but nothing would save him from me.

Plaza Hotel, Victoria Island, 8:30pm

Eddie punched in the aide's number and waited for a response. He glanced at his brother and smiled. Benny was just cleaning up his tools – pliers, scissors, knives, stuff like that. She had been a bit difficult but, in the end, they always squeal. She didn't have the photo; they confirmed that after ransacking the place but at least they had a name and a number. Suleiman picked up and Eddie told him that Debola had given the photo to a guy called Edwin 'Caesar' Clark. Suleiman suddenly became agitated and told him he would get back to him.

Senator Kuti's Residence, Abuja, 8:32am

The two naked bodies writhed and trashed about on the bed until finally they pushed away from each other. Senator Kuti sat up and picked up a glass of red wine from the bedside table. He sipped slowly, relishing the drink and also relishing the sight of Cassandra Okafor's taut, glistening body. It filled him with pleasure to know that he was the one ravishing such a voluptuous, desirable woman.

'Hmm, that was great,' murmured Cassandra, 'Better than the last round and that was fantastic too.'

'Well don't give me all the credit. You really do like to take it in the rear, don't you? I guessed so, from the way you moaned.'

'Don't be so smug!' she said laughing.

Senator Kuti was young, well-built and quite an attractive man. He looked nothing like his pot-bellied colleagues at the Senate House. He stroked his goatee thoughtfully as he contemplated his lover. She was nothing like her colleagues either.

His land line phone was ringing in his study. Frowning, he padded over naked to answer it, while Cassandra purred and stretched like a big cat.

'Hello?' he asked in a gruff voice.

'It's Suleiman on the line. We're in big trouble.'

'How?'

'Caesar's got the photo.'

There was a heavy silence for a few seconds that felt like eternity.

Senator Kuti glanced furtively over his shoulder to make sure that Cassandra was still in the bedroom. He had to breathe in slowly to calm his accelerated heart rate.

'Give them Caesar's file,' he said at last, 'Tell them to make him disappear. The Boss must never know about this or we are all dead. When they are done, hire a separate unit to take them out. Make sure there are no loose ends.'

'Yes, Sir.'

'Get it done.'

Federal Palace Hotel, Victoria Island, 8:58pm

The Bucho Brothers met up with Suleiman who gave them a file and proceeded to explain things to them and answer questions.

Eddie exclaimed when he saw the photograph of Caesar and showed it to Benny who exclaimed as well.

'It's the fag! There really is a good, kind God.'

'You bet!' Eddie said grinning. He turned to Suleiman who asked what he was missing.

'Never mind that, it's just a private joke. Is the target dangerous?'

'No, not really but he carries a weapon: a Browning 9mm pistol. He hasn't shot anyone with it though, as far as we know.

'As you can see from the photo, he's tall and handsome, six feet tall, slim build, dark honey-coloured complexion, eyes brown. He's very fashionable, likes to dress well and maintains a flashy lifestyle. He smokes incessantly, drinks a lot and loves women, especially those of questionable character. He supports his lifestyle with money from his mother, who happens to be the current Minister of Aviation, Cassandra Chiamaka Okafor. They have a thorny relationship. His father is Barrister Edward Clark who is currently separated from his wife. He lives in London.

'He is smart, cunning with a total disregard of the risks of his trade and, unless he is killed, he won't stop being a nuisance.'

'Okay' Eddie seemed satisfied and slightly intrigued, 'Is there anything else we should know about him?'

'Yeah. Remember the Kebby Creek killings?'

'Yes, it was all over the news about six years ago.'

'He was the one that exposed the people responsible. One of them is still at large. Also there is another incident that happened a year before that; it made Caesar somewhat of a celebrity. Remember Peter Marquis?'

'The Billionaire playboy-politician? He was murdered by some psychopath, right?'

'She is known as Mel 'The Butcherette' Thatcher. Our man actually met her. I hear he's the only one who has seen her face and lived to tell the tale.'

'He seems a lucky bastard.'

'That's what I'm worried about. You have to kill him at all costs.'

'Oh, don't worry. He'll need far more than luck to escape us. He'll need nothing short of a bloody miracle.'

Caesar's Apartment, Lekki, 9:30pm

I hear a car pull up and I wonder whether he has finally arrived. I resist the urge to peep through the window because the lights are on and I don't want to risk him seeing me. I hear a pair of footsteps approaching and they stop in front of the front door. Did Caesar bring a friend? I'm sorry I've waited far too long for this moment and so his friend will have to die too. I crouch behind the sofa and my heart beats with excitement. At last, I will have my revenge.

'That's odd,' said Eddie as he stared at the lock on Caesar's door 'This lock's been tampered with. There are scratches all over it.'

'Maybe he lost his key' said Benny with a shrug, 'Hurry up, let's go in and make ourselves comfortable. His car is not outside.'

He cased the corridor while Eddie skillfully sprung the lock with a sharp click.

Both of them were dressed in dark clothes and carried knapsacks. Inside were tools of their trade which included ropes, chains, machetes, knives, ice picks and machine tools. They had absolutely no interest in firearms.

Making their way into the living room they silently surveyed the quarters.

'This guy sure knows how to live!' Benny exclaimed enviously as he stared with awe at the plasma TV.

Eddie grunted.

'Big deal. It's a good thing he enjoyed his life because it ends tonight. Now where do we hide?'

Benny's answer was interrupted by a loud, bloodcurdling yell and a figure leaped out from behind a sofa, brandishing a huge knife.

'What the...' Eddie started in disbelief as the attacker descended on him.

The knife came down with a flash and he had no choice but to use his arm to block it. The razor sharp blade sank into his forearm with a sickening thunk and he screamed in agony. He lashed out with his foot and caught his assailant in the stomach. The figure crumpled up on the floor, retching.

'Eddie! Are you okay?' cried Benny in concern.

'I'm bleeding profusely' said Eddie with a grimace, 'Do I look okay?'

'It's a woman' remarked Benny incredulously.

The younger Bucho pulled the lady up by her hair. She tried to claw at his face and he slapped her hard. She went down again.

'Who is this madwoman?' asked Eddie curiously, 'Caesar's girlfriend?'

'I don't think so.'

They watched with mild interest as she struggled to get to her feet. She really did look crazy. She was wearing black jeans and a black halter top that looked like they hadn't been washed in weeks. A pair of torn, black knock-off sneakers was on her feet. Her hair was scattered and unkempt and she smelled of stale sweat. But what intrigued the brothers the most were her face.

She wasn't pretty but she wasn't ugly either. Her skin was jet black, even darker than her clothes. Then her eyes. They were huge and cat-like, pupils as black as midnight gleamed from yellow irises. She looked like a creature from another dimension. Even the sadistic brothers were rattled by the intense hatred that blazed in those portals. There was absolutely no fear in them.

She made to spring at them like a wildcat and they grabbed her again. She struggled wildly, clawing and spitting furiously. She took sizable chunk of Benny's cheek under her long, sharp fingernails.

'Bitch!' he swore and punched her, again and again, 'What do we do with her?'

'Well I guess we'll have to kill her.'

'But Suleiman is only paying us for Caesar's murder.'

'She's already seen our faces and the neighbours might have heard something. Let's tie her up and put her in the boot. We have to get out of here.'

'Then what?' Benny couldn't hide the eagerness in his voice.

'We have a long night ahead of us' Eddie said with a smile, 'We can always get Caesar another day.'

Senator Kuti's Residence, Abuja, August 19, 2008, 10:30am

The senator walked around the compound of his immense mansion and lovingly inspected the beautiful flowers that adorned the gardens. Senator Kuti loved flowers. They brought a sense of peace and harmony to his otherwise dark and chaotic life. He took in their fragrance, widening his nostrils as he filled his lungs. He felt happy.

However, the serenity of his mid-morning reverie was shattered as a figure wearing a traditional long, white caftan burst through the open gates and ran towards him holding what looked like a newspaper in his hand.

The senator's eyes narrowed. It was Suleiman. He looked very harassed.

'What?!' snapped Kuti, 'Didn't I tell you not to disturb me?'

'This is yesterday's edition of *Scoop* Magazine. I tried to call you but you switched off your phone. I just flew in.' Suleiman knew why the senator's phone was switched off. Some poor lady was probably chained to his bed.

Kuti opened the folded paper and the headlines jumped out and hit him in the eyes:

HUMAN TRAFFICKING RING EXPOSED! SENATOR SIMON KUTI WANTED FOR MURDER

'Goddam it!' screamed Kuti 'He was just one man. How could you fools let him do this to me?'

'I told you we shouldn't have hired the Buchos. Those sick bastards screwed everything up.'

'I have to get out of here' the senator said, suddenly scared, 'The Boss might have set the dogs loose.'

As if on cue, there was a loud roar as a jeep made its way through the gates and towards the two men.

'NO!' screeched Suleiman, 'They're here! They've come to kill us!'

The two men scampered towards the house. Too late. The jeep pulled up alongside the fleeing, terrified men and the side windows rolled down. The following second, the long ugly snouts of machine pistols fitted with silencers jutted out. There were rapid coughs and the men buckled and fell. More shots were fired at the prone bodies. The jeep made a U-turn and took off.

The assassin in the back seat dialed a number.

Undisclosed location, 10:36am

She picked up the phone on the second ring.

'Hello?' her voice was curt and cold.

'It's done.'

'Both of them?'

'Yes.'

A pause.

'Good work. Find the Bucho Brothers and get rid of them. Find them, torture them and kill them. I want them to be used as an example of what happens to anyone who tries to carry out a hit that is not sanctioned by me. Let the cops find the bodies.'

'Yes, Boss.'

'I want you to dismantle the entire operation. There's going to be too much heat now. Pay off all the girls involved. Warn them that anyone who talks will be severely dealt with. Understood?'

'Yes, Boss. What about Caesar?'

Another pause.

'No one touches him. Nobody makes a move on him unless I say so. We can't risk making him a martyr. That could jeopardize our other interests.'

'Yes, Boss.'

'Now get to work.'

She hung up.

She placed the phone on the dressing table and stared at her reflection in the mirror for a long time. She picked up a framed photograph and studied the portrait. It was a picture of a young, ravishing woman holding a beautiful five year old boy on her lap. They looked strikingly similar and both looked very happy and content.

She sighed and gently touched the boy's image through the glass. What a handsome boy he was, she thought. Why was he so stubborn?

She knew the answer. Her son was everything she was: beautiful, intelligent, and stubborn, with a total disregard of rules. He was her spawn, what else did she expect? One day, one of them would have to succumb to the other.

Yeah, right.

*

It's a long, straight, wide road to hell and soon I will be there with you my sweet sister. Will God ever forgive us for the things we did? I don't think so.

It's ironic I should die horribly in the hands of these foul men. You suffered the same fate only that it was me that was your tormentor. I had planned to mete out the same punishment to another but yet again he slipped through my fingers. Caesar seems to have the luck of the devil.

Will you forgive me my dear sister? As eternal fire consumes our souls, will you be there for me? Can we suffer our damnation together? Could things have been different, had we discussed our problems together, like a family? I guess it doesn't matter. It's what was meant to be.

We are the products of this cold world, the children of fate, the daughters of Eve, a wasted generation. And I hope that, if there is another life after this, we can be a true family, running and playing in gardens filled with flowers and chasing butterflies, where true love never dies.

LIGHTLESS ROOM
Jumoke Verissimo

There was never light in the room when she visited and he never said anything about the darkness. Every evening, they talked into the night, stopping only when his grandfather clock chimed twelve times, announcing midnight. Then, he'd say in a sleepy drawl which sounded like that of a bored, underpaid actor:

'You should get going now.'

Initially, the lightless room had not bothered her, until she started getting edgy in there. Her nervousness heightened when he changed his sitting position and there was a fleeting brush on her skin, or when their brief silence turned into a stifled desire, and when he exhaled to ease the silence, the tepid air from his nostril dabbing and caressing her skin wickedly. At these times, she confined her emotions into a blob of spit and she swallowed slowly, rather than let out the moans that had clogged her throat. She always felt like a never-lit hurricane lantern rusting away at these times.

'I'll switch on the lights this evening,' she mumbled her thoughts, as she walked past his house. She was on her way to the campus. She stopped a few steps away from his house, and stared fixedly at it. His curtains were so closed together, no light could stream into the room. Her mobile phone rang at this time, and she ignored it. She gazed continuously at his shut windows. She allowed her mind to wander into the dark room, and she recalled a smell of rust, a lingering muskiness and diffused dust. A car horn jolted her, and she walked on, slowly at first, then her steps gaining a steady momentum as this led her to the turning at the end of the street. She stopped at this junction and turned to look at the house one last time. She sighed, sifted her thoughts, and wondered aloud again:

'What colour is that room? Are the walls painted blue, green or gray or are they painted at all? Did it have wallpaper with flowers on it?'

When she began to feel edgy in the room, she promised herself several times, never to go back to his dark room, but it was with passion that she re-enacted her visit to his house each evening, where they sat in the dark and talked about everything, except putting the lights on.

*

The evening of that day, in his lightless room, she leaned on the chair; her head was against the wall, while the rest of her remained in the chair as she thought of how she could light the room. She moved her hands to the wall and felt the protruding button of the switch, her hands lingered for a while and she mustered courage to push it down but her hand slipped back to a position of idleness by her thigh.

Once, she felt she was confident enough and said, 'please put the lights on. It is dark in here.' She explained that she wanted to see what he looked like after his long imprisonment.

'Have you brightened from seeing no sunray or flaked into layers of dead cells?'

She closed her eyes in anticipation. When she opened them, it was still dark and she hadn't asked any question. Finally, she found the courage to ask him why there was *never* light in the room. He said: 'The colour of the room makes me nervous.'

'Change it. I will get a painter tomorrow.'

'I can't.'

'Why?' he heaved a sigh and was silent for some long seconds.

'I think there's value in the dark and lights will consume it.' She got no sense out of his talk. He paused for her to agree and when she didn't, he said, 'Don't you know, sometimes, it is best to be in the dark, to be in a vacuum; that vacuum will become the reason of our existence. It will give meaning to our lives as we will seek to fill *it* – that emptiness – the rest of our lives.' Again, he paused, waiting for her to talk, and when she failed to take the cue, he continued,

'The hope of filling the vacuum keeps us. Don't you agree?' He didn't wait for her response this time, before he added quickly,

'Let's remain in the dark.'

She decided she wouldn't care about the darkness in the room anymore, or the changes he had had over the years. She leaned against the chair, and heard the droning of his metallic voice, but not his talk.

*

The first day she visited him because she had bet with her roommate that she could go to his house in order to find out if he had gone crazy after his return from prison, as the rumours said. However, the untold truth was that she had gone to him out of personal desire and not because of money staked. His derangement story gained ground among his neighbours because he never left the house, except when he visited the neighbourhood market, once a week, wearing a cloth that covered him like a burqa.

He was a troublesome academic whom the government wanted to get rid of, but never did. In fact, he escaped many imprisoning attempts, until he crowned his advocacy with a revived childhood grudge for the head-of-state at a National Economic Emancipation Conference. At the event, the head-of-state moved from one seat to another, greeting participants and he had stopped to exchange pleasantries with him too. The head-of-state smiled at him with an outstretched hand, and he leaned forward as if he was about to return the gesture with a hearty handshake, only to punch the number one man, fully, on the face. It was on live TV. The head-of-state was popeyed and still. Nobody moved for some seconds, not even the head-of-state's security men. Suddenly, the shock wore off the security men rushed him, and bundled him out of the venue into a waiting Black Maria. As they carried him out of the hall he screamed into the microphone a TV reporter held out.

'That was the only opportunity I had to retaliate what that bully did to me while we were in secondary school and is still doing to me now that he is head-of-state!'

The first day she visited him, she knocked on his door for about ten minutes and was almost turning back when he opened it, slightly. No part of him showed through the small opening.

'May I help you?'

'I – I – I am your neighbour…'

'So?'

She was rooted in fear. She pondered over her coming as his eyes glistened in the darkness like a cat's. When she discovered that she was unable to contest his stare, she turned to leave.

'Young woman, you must have a reason for coming to my doorstep at this time of the day.'

She stopped, but made no response. She had a reason but she didn't remember it. She wanted to say something. She said nothing. She turned around, faced him, yet remained at same spot. He assessed her. She waited. His brows deepened. He had not spoken to anyone in three weeks.

'What do you do?' He finally asked, clearing his throat simultaneously.

'I am a student at the University of Ibadan.'

'That was my university for many years, you know, but… anyway…' He unhooked the door latch and let her in without any invitation.

That first day, the light was off and she didn't ask him to put *his* lights on. As they talked, she imagined his features in the darkness. His presence awed her. And when she laughed at the jokes he made, it sounded like the squeaking of a mouse with a sore throat. On that first day, the darkness hid her fidgets. She welcomed its defence.

Since then, they held discussions in the lightless room. He talked about everything that intrigued her – about politics, culture, economics, history and then about his past activism, but he avoided any talk of him turning the lights on. Many times there was a part of them that ached for that stuff that could happen in the dark, between a diffident woman and a wanting man.

*

She moved her forefinger on the chair, absentmindedly.

'So you understand me now? You have to understand the way these things work.' He said, rapping the arm of his chair.

'…we cannot grow until we germinate a democracy that is home-grown.'

She heard some, but not his entire sentence, and when she tried making sense of what she heard it didn't add up. She could not stop thinking of how much she wanted the room lit. She imagined his skin under the lights and spit streamed into her mouth. This time she didn't swallow it.

'Where is the toilet?' Her voice quivered and she tried not to splash the spit in her mouth on him as she talked.

'Are you okay?'

She swallowed some spit and grunted, 'Yes.'

'Ok then. Use your mobile phone to see the way in the corridor. It is the last room on your right.'

She swung her hand as she walked past him, so the dull lights of the phone could light a part of his face. He shifted to a side, as she walked past and the light from the phone fell on the arm of the chair. She hit her leg against an object, she mumbled, and then she manoeuvred herself into the room, carefully.

*

He sat, chin-in-hand, waiting, ruminating over her visits of the previous days. She was his most frequent visitor since his return from prison and he enjoyed her company. She never asked him too many questions. She listened. He liked her that way. Listening. The only question he remembered her asking was who did his housecleaning, and she had laughed unconcernedly when he said it was his hobby to wash the toilet and sweep his rooms. She hadn't even asked if he did everything in the dark.

He loved her voice. It brought back memories that he should not necessarily connect her with. The first day she came to the house, she reminded him of the clumsiness of his first day in class. The next, she was the anticipation of his favourite food, and every other day, she became something he looked forward to knowing.

She walked back into the sitting room, flashing the dull light of the phone in his direction. He shifted to a side, for her to pass, and the lights from the phone fell on the arm of the chair. She sat dispirited, resting her head against the wall, and then her hands moved towards what felt like a switch. This time, she was aware of her action. Her hands remained on the switch as he talked about the government's new policies. Her hands lingered on the switch as he lambasted the nation's problems on the colonial masters who fused different ethnic groups into a state.

What is the worst that can happen if I switch the lights on? She thought as she removed her hand from the switch.

The grandfather clock ticked continuously and when it was 11.30pm it chimed loudly, a preparatory for midnight. The clock chimed every half-hour, and it had been one of the things that had amused her at the onset. Now it disturbed her.

She shifted to the edge of the chair in readiness for taking her leave.

'It is almost twelve.' She said, as if it was a soliloquy. Again, you fail, she thought, and for a moment she struggled with herself in order not to flick the switch.

'I have to leave now.' She picked her words. Her voice was low yet audible.

'Are you tired already? Usually, I am the one who prompts you to leave.'

She wanted to tell him how tired she was of being in the dark. That she knew all his political dispositions, and she had heard them too many times. That she knew the order of his words when he wanted to begin a sentence. She wanted to say, maybe if he put the lights on, the somberness which hung over him would go away too. She didn't. She didn't state the reasons she was leaving before he prompted her – as on other days. She stood up and walked towards the door, wordlessly.

'I get it, you are tired of me… I was going to tell you this anyway. I leave for Canada next week. I have been offered a job.' He wasn't going to take the job, but he said it. He wanted to say something that would provoke her reaction. He didn't want her to leave. For a moment they did not exchange any word. They hid their thoughts in the darkness.

'We still have a month to see each other then.' She said. He felt let down – disappointed. She smiled without cause. It was the only form of expression that came to her then, but he didn't see it. She wanted to tell him they had never seen each other aside from their meeting on the first day, and even that memory was of a voice not a man, but all she did was keeping a gambol smile.

She walked to the door and raised her hands to find the doorknob. She waited for him to beg her to stay, that he would put the lights on. She lingered for a while, contemplating opening the door or convincing him to light the room. Finally she said:

'It's okay. We will see each other again.'

'Stay for a while.'

'I don't like staying in this darkness.' She voiced finally.

The clock chimed, one… two… three… it struck twelve as if it was the parting note. She moved to the door and opened it.

'See-you-to-mo-rrow.' He said in monosyllables.

'Yes, see you tomorrow…' And then she sneered, '…in the dark.' It was at the tip of her tongue, but she didn't say it. She heard the click of his door as she walked down the stairs.

She remained at the end of the stairs crying. The tears that coursed down her cheeks from her eyes formed a salty stream on her upper lips. She leaned on the banister at the end of the stairs and cast a long look at the house, before deciding it would be her last visit. This time she decided she would never come back.

In the early days of her visit, she had enjoyed everything; the awe of *him* sharing his political views with her, had made her ignore the room's darkness. But the lightlessness now abetted an emotion that tugged at the muscles in her abdomen. The meeting was mere curiosity at first, but it became an anticipation that metamorphosed into something that defied all the words she had accumulated in her lifetime. She sat down on the last stairs. I should never have come here to see him. I should have left him in my fantasies.

She lingered for a while on the stairs before she stood up.

*

He heard the fading sound of her footsteps as she climbed down the stairs. He leaned against the doorpost. *Open the door.* He prompted himself. He didn't. Instead he walked to the light switch with fidgeting hands, and then he leaned against the wall, building his courage to push down the button. His middle finger rested against the switch in a slack, and then it became rigid against the button, he pressed hard and the lights came on. He flipped the lights on, and then off, and on again. He sighed. He stood with his back against the wall staring at the bulb. He moved away from the wall, and he moved back and leaned on it, and he began flicking the switch on and off with his index finger. He moved closer to the bulb and stared at it lengthily. Nothing happened to him.

He reflected on their parting. She had broken the routine. She had questioned him. She had asked him to switch the lights on. She had decided when to leave for home. Fear gripped him as he stared at the wall. He felt like a vacuum. There had been a noticeable lack of lustre in her voice. He switched off the light hoping that, by the time the darkness returned, she would be there, but after a long wait without hearing her breath whisper, he walked to the switch and turned the lights on again. Her not coming back to his house after that day jolted him as he thought of her forthcoming absence. The house became desolate and dark. He stared at the colour of the wall which he had once used as his defence, picked up his T-shirt, swung it over his shoulder and rushed out of the room, opening the door with force.

When he got out of the house on the stair-head, he realised that he didn't know her house. He had never asked her, all those times she had visited him. All he knew was that she was a neighbour from one of the clustered, low-cost houses in the neighbourhood.

The mellow light of the 60 watts bulb that lit the exterior of his house shone brightly. The cold wind blew against his skin and he folded his hands into a criss-cross over his shoulders. He leaned on the banister and looked down to where she stood like a child who had lost a prized pencil on her first day in school and he imagined that when she sighted him, she would let out a sigh.

Pretending that he was oblivious of her, he watched her walk up the stairs with shaky legs, while she gripped the banister for support until she got to the landing.

He stood directly in front of her wanting to say words that would soothe, but facing her, he said everything with a stare.

'You…' He finally said.

'You…' She replied. And they both burst into a long laugh. He turned, and moved towards the door. She remained a step behind him but their hands remained in a lock. It was when he got to the door that he released her hand, and walked into the room ahead of her. She remained at the door.

'There is light in the room. Please. Come in.' It was his first real invitation to her. 'There will always be lights. Light, no more darkness…' She put the tip of her index finger to his lips. 'Shh…'

For a while, he noticed her questioning look, as she took in the colour of the room – brown. *Why brown?* A bookshelf with so many fat books faced the door directly. There was no television. A small Phillips transistor radio was plugged into a socket close to it. It stood on a small table a few metres from the shelf. The colour of his Persian rug was a black-red mix. The grandfather clock stood by his chair. She paused for a moment and looked at him against the light. His skin appeared iridescent.

He watched her walk into the room and walk about the room, dazed. When she caught his stare, she looked away. But he had looked away too. He stole glances at her cocoa-skin. The beauty of a dark skin which glimmered against the electric-light bulb caught his attention. He smiled to himself, knowingly. I have conquered fear. I have conquered darkness. He held her hand and they walked around the lit room, wordless.

*

When he opened his eyes, he was alone in the darkness. His right hand stretched out, and his fist clasped in a grip as if he was holding her, but he held nothing. She was not with him.

PAY DAY
Ifeanyi Ogboh

Dawn was approaching. A cock crowed twice some distance away and soon the muezzin would be heard, calling all the faithful to the day's first prayers. There had not been electricity in the vicinity for a week and the residents had lost all hope of it, as there were rumours that the transformer would have to be taken away.

Ignatius carried a bucket of water to the bathroom. He always had his bath early, as his co-tenants in the *face-me-I-face-you* knew. But today he had it earlier. After a quick five-minute bath in the cramped bathroom that all the tenants used, he dashed to his room and hurriedly changed into the clothes that had been neatly placed on the chair. His alacrity was like that of a soldier rushing for a parade. In three minutes he had combed his hair, dressed fully and even knotted a black tie on his white shirt.

As the solitary candle in his room flickered, he picked up the CD placed on the bed and opened the case to be sure it was the right one. It was labelled with permanent blue ink: PAY-DAY. He slipped it into a small envelope, blew out the candle and emerged from his quarters. As he stepped out on the street in a quick trot, the muezzin started its cry and he knew it was 5 a.m.

Ignatius got to the bus-stop after about ten minutes. There was a middle-aged lady waiting. Even though he had a tie, she looked at him suspiciously. He ignored her brazen stare and looked out for a bus, tightly clutching his envelope. After a while, a *molue* approached with the conductor shouting 'Oshodi! Oshodi!' Ignatius quickly boarded it, although it barely stopped to pick its fares. His journey had begun.

When he arrived at Oshodi, it was almost seven o'clock and the place was already a madhouse with commuters and vehicles moving helter-skelter. He went to a taxi park and haggled for a ride to Akin

Adesola Street on the Island.

'How much?'

'1,000 naira.'

'You won't take 200 naira?'

The cabbie frowned and looked away. He spat out and said, '700 naira, last price.'

'I can't pay you more than 400 naira. In short, I'll take a bus', and he stormed away.

'*Oga, Oga*, please, come back.' Ignatius turned around.

'OK, I will take you…'

Ignatius smiled as he got into the taxi, knowing that his bluff had paid off.

When they got to Victoria Island, he realized that the taxi driver didn't know the street, as he had claimed. After stopping and asking a few people, they finally got to Ignatius destination: Octan & Phillips, consultant engineers. It was a neat five-storey building. He paid the driver and entered the building. It was 8.00 a.m..

'I'd like to see Mr. Phillips,' he said to the receptionist.

'Do you have an appointment?'

'Yes, tell him it's Mr Imodibo, Ignatius Imodibo.'

'Please, hold on a moment,' she said as she clutched the receiver, her long nails, like the talons of an eagle, encircling it.

'Sir, a Mr Ignatius Imodibo says he has an appointment with Mr Phillips.' She quickly hung up the phone and led him to the lift.

'Fifth floor, just go straight down,' she directed.

Shortly afterwards, Ignatius was in a large office, sparsely furnished but with a lot of taste. It was covered with a soft blue carpet from wall to wall. There was a small conference table in the room, in the middle of which sat a vase, four chairs were placed neatly around the table. A small bookshelf stood unobtrusively in one corner. On one of the walls there was a large woven tapestry showcasing what looked like a map of Lagos. The opposite end was all glass, offering a breathtaking view of the lagoon. All the furniture screamed class.

Mr Phillips was staring at the view his large windows afforded. He turned as Ignatius entered.

'So, Ignatius, I hope you have something good for me.'

'Yes, sir,' he said as he retrieved the CD from the envelope.

Someone came in behind Ignatius.

'That is Peter Owu. He handles our new IT department now. I

will value his opinion in this matter.'

Ignatius turned to shake his hand.

'I think we have met before,' he said.

'Oh, really, I can't place the face,' Peter responded.

'The last time I came here you were at the visitors' waiting room. Remember, I told you I was a programmer, and you gave me some words of advice.'

'I vaguely remember, that day was a really busy day.'

'As all days are, let us get down to business quickly,' Mr Phillips cut in.

The three converged round a small table. Peter placed a laptop he had brought with him on the table.

'So, let's see what you have', Peter said, with a lisp.

'For this thing to work well, the computer needs to be connected to the internet.'

Peter raised an eyebrow. Mr Phillips nodded in agreement. That wasn't a problem.

'It is, go on,' he said.

Ignatius opened the case, retrieved the CD and placed it in the CD-ROM drive of the laptop. The disc started spinning as he bit his lips in expectation. He was tense but he tried not to show it. Beethoven's ninth symphony filled the room as the screen flickered. A digital clock appeared in the middle of the screen, showing that the program was still loading. It started its countdown: 10-9-8-7-6-5-4-3-2-1...

The screen was suddenly filled with splashes of colour as Ignatius announced:

'This is Proteus Pro, an integrated virtual office software that allows you to keep tabs on the progress of all aspects of the office, to update jobs and to source help on anything online. It allows different users to see different things depending on the level of control you want that user to have. There are links to Accounts, Human Resources, Engineering Department, Site Managers, Projects, Marketing, Clients and the Web. All of his has been designed as you requested. As it is going to be online, the workers can update their own job schedules and tie them to the bonuses they are meant to receive. Also, it enables you to see that the clients are never behind schedule as there is a link between level of progress and payments made, telling you which are behind schedule, which deadlines have not been met by the workers, etcetera....'

He showed them the links as he worked his way through the site. He felt his voice sounded dry and hoarse because he was still tense, so he tried to relax by talking slowly. He had been working on this project for close to a year now. Initially, his mentor and friend, Mark, had gotten the job after lobbying for a while. Ignatius had met Mark in unusual circumstances. He had got a job as an office cleaner in his secondary school in order to earn some money during the holidays. The cleaning company sent him to fill in for one of the cleaners in an IT firm. While there, he had met Mark, a university student also doing a part-time job. Mark was a burgeoning programmer, working on some pet projects. However, he lacked the patience to do some easy but tedious calculations. He had been looking for someone to pass the buck to. Ignatius was willing to learn, and he learnt fast. They kept in touch even after Ignatius stopped working in the cleaning firm and Mark had gone back to school. Now with Mark, Ignatius earned money selling petty programs that were assignments for university students. He was always welcome in Mark's home. Few people knew that Ignatius was still in secondary school. He looked much older than his real age. When the jobs increased in number, Ignatius started skipping school. Soon, he felt it was irrelevant. When they got a contract to do Proteus Pro for Octan & Phillips, Ignatius dropped out of school in the first term of SS3. He needed all the time he could get. Now he worked in a cyber café. He knew that if this worked, he could get any other IT job he wanted because they had tried to integrate so many things into this one. In fact, Octan & Phillips had been using a limited version of the software for six months already. They had not completed it yet, so they gave them a demo to try out. So far, Mr Phillips had not been won over by it. Mark had gotten fed up after that and a postgraduate scholarship to study in Ireland had suddenly bailed him out three months before. Ignatius, now alone, was still determined to see it through.

'Why don't you give it up and look for a scholarship to leave this country?' Mark had counselled.

'I like finishing everything I start,' Ignatius replied through gritted teeth. 'Besides, I really think that this job can make me a king in this country.'

Ignatius knew that Octan & Phillips had found his program very useful, especially as it integrated software that made the time-consuming engineering calculations easier, enabling them to perform more jobs more quickly. However, they had to pretend they didn't like it in order to allow them to negotiate a low price for the package. They had not received a dime since the initial 50,000 naira advance handed over at the beginning of the project which had now dragged on for a whole year instead of the initially agreed six months. He now had to work nights in a cyber café, to earn his keep, and share his daytime between working on this project and sleeping. He always wondered how he managed to live from day to day. It wasn't his fault that the contract had been extended. Mr Phillips had kept on suggesting more and more things to the extent that it now seemed like a never-ending project. Then, he had forced him to give him a final and definitive list of desired modifications, so that the project would come to an end and he would receive the final 250,000 naira severance pay. He had some doubts about Mr Phillips making good his own part of the deal, as he always seemed to find fault with whatever was presented to him. This, however, was to be the last visit he was to make here, he promised himself.

'Okay, we will deploy it for another two weeks, then I will pay you the balance,' Mr Phillips concluded after the demonstration and question-and-answer session. This time around, surprisingly, he had left most of the questions to Peter. Peter had only asked some elementary questions about the architecture of the portal: questions that did anything but rattle him. They simply betrayed how little Peter knew about the project, as most of the measures he wanted in place had been well taken care of.

'But I thought you had tried it for long enough; after all, I was only making slight modifications which you now seem to be satisfied with. I need the money, badly. I deserve it.'

'Yes, you deserve it, but nobody gives out money for merchandise that he has doubts about. You should know that. Just two weeks,' he said with a tone of finality.

He was shown out. As he passed the reception, the receptionist was engrossed in a society gossip magazine and barely raised her head.

He came out onto the road again. He thought that he would be walking on air after collecting his cheque and would indulge himself by taking a cab to go home. Now he didn't even feel capable to board a bus. It was a bright day with the sun glorious in the sky but it might as well have been a dark rainy night to him in his gloom. He walked down the street, ignoring buses calling Obalende, which he should have boarded. He just needed time to cool off, to simmer down the anger that boiled within him. He had woken up that day with a lot of excitement, but the climax had turned to an anti-climax and it pissed him off. Two weeks seemed like an eternity, as he had been stalled for too long.

He was lost in thought and didn't notice a guy running towards him from a side street. Before he knew what was happening, he was with the guy, on the floor in a heap.

'Oh, sorry. I am very sorry that I didn't see you,' the young man who ran into him apologised profusely.

He pulled Ignatius up and dusted him down. Ignatius was still in angst-land all this while. He didn't even notice the man beat the dust off his clothes.

'Sorry sir,' the young man kept repeating.

'No problem.' Ignatius finally managed to mutter, to reassure the man that his entreaties had not fallen on deaf ears.

The man soon disappeared in a flash, running in the same direction that he had been in before the accident.

Ignatius walked on. Then, he felt his pocket. His wallet and mobile phone were gone.

There was a lot of activity at the bus park at Ojota that afternoon. Many buses speeding on the expressway screeched briefly under the pedestrian bridge to discharge their passengers before moving on, calling their destinations in their wake. Motor park boys criss-crossed the road, grabbing the bags of people whom they believed to be travelling and conveying them quickly to their bus of choice: each one wanted his bus to be the first to be filled, so fierce was the competition. Some of their victims struggled to have their bags back while others just gave in. There were two policemen stationed on one side of the road, ready to apprehend anybody who, failing to use the overhead bridge, decided to cross the expressway. However, they never seemed to be able to catch the touts – or they didn't dare to. Hawkers were everywhere, carrying all kinds of wares from toothbrushes to whisky, meandering in the throng of pedestrians heading in different directions.

Cordelia was like a misfit in this throng. She kept on obstructing people because she could not be in as much of a hurry as they were. She didn't know where to go because this was her first time in Lagos. All she had was an address and a description. However, she had to ask for information on which bus to take. Before she left the village, she had been told to be wary of Lagosians. She'd heard all sorts of stories about people selling their souls for money and using other people to make *juju*. She stopped by a woman selling roasted plantain by the roadside. Surely this woman would look kindly towards her.

'Excuse me ma. I am looking for where I can get a bus to Oshodi.'

The plantain woman looked up at her and then looked down again at her wares as if she was not being talked to.

Cordelia repeated her plea.

The woman now looked up at her again, sized her up and pointed to her right, without saying a word. Cordelia went off in that direction. She got to a place where there were some buses preparing to leave and asked the touts there which of the buses was going to Oshodi. The touts thought for a moment and then one of them said: 'Ah, sister, go down this way then cross the road over there. Then you will see the bus to Oshodi.'

He pointed in the direction she had just come from. She did as he said. When she got to the point indicated, she asked again. This time, she asked an ice-cream vendor. He made as if he didn't understand English. She then repeated the request in Igbo. The vendor's face lit up and he pointed out the location of the bus to Oshodi: it was just behind them. Then he added, in Igbo: 'Nne, why didn't you speak Igbo to me the first time.'

She didn't know what to say in reply so she just thanked him and quickly boarded the bus before it zoomed off.

*

Peter was impressed with what he saw. It seemed that each time he viewed the program, there was always more to discover, an endless vista. He was so impressed that he became jealous of Ignatius. He'd been told to deploy the program on the company's network. They had successfully been using the limited version of the program, for the previous three months. But it was nothing compared to what he had just been given. He suspected that Mr Phillips was planning to cheat Ignatius, but that wasn't his business anyway.

Suddenly, the screen went black. He checked the power cord: it was still connected. He traced the power supply from the socket on the wall to the computer: everything seemed in order. He now switched off the monitor and switched it back on. But there was only a blue background with a message flashing: call 08062424241. The phone rang. He picked it up. It was Mr Phillips. He had the same problem on his computer in the network: the same message flashing and nothing else. Peter promised to look into it and to report back immediately: a temporary glitch in the network, he assured. As soon as he hung up the phone, it rang again. It was the accounts department: same problem. Two other calls in quick succession, all with the same problem. He restarted the computer. A message box came up before it started booting: enter password or call 08062424241. The problem could only have one cause.

Soon after, Mr Phillips called again and asked him to report to his office immediately. Peter knew he had to give a very good explanation for what was going on. He walked into Mr Philips's office slowly, deliberating on what he would say when he got there. Mr Phillips's secretary, a slim, young lady, waved him past.

'What is wrong with the network, Peter?' she asked as he grabbed the door handle. 'This has never happened before.'

'It's just this new program they got. It's just a temporary thing,' Peter replied, unconvincingly, as he opened the door to the office. The boss was seated in his chair, directly facing the door. In one of the visitors' seats was Mr Dele Durojaiye, the admin manager.

'What took you so long? So what is the situation with this thing?' Mr Phillips badgered.

'I was trying to crack the codes of the program that is causing all of these problems. The guy is an amateur so it should not take much time. Forget about the threat of calling the number.'

'So, Dele, did you try the number on the screen?' Mr Phillips asked as if Peter had not spoken.

'Yes. It rang but nobody picked the phone. Maybe we should try again.'

'Yes, I think so. But you should also start looking for this boy. He can't be holding us to ransom like this. And Peter, do break that code. I pay you good money to handle these things.'

'Yes sir.'

'I want two of you on this. If you don't get through over the phone, ask around and find where he works, where he hangs out, where he sleeps. In fact, call in the police. Just find him fast. We have a big project for the federal government to deliver this week and the boys, who are already behind schedule, can't deliver with all their systems down. We are losing big money here and your jobs could be on the line. Is that clear?'

They nodded vigorously in unison and quickly left the office.

'So what do you intend to do?' Peter asked the admin manager after they had left the office.

'Well, I will try and find his house while I keep trying his number. Or do you know where he lives? I will check the files, he must have put a contact address in the initial project proposal. Are you coming with me?'

'No. I think we can crack this program. This guy has not done many jobs. In fact, from what I heard, he's a secondary school drop-out, so he can't be that good. I would rather work on it while you try to find him,' Peter said as he walked to his office. Then, he suddenly turned round when he got to his door and walked back towards Dele. He had remembered something.

'If you insist on finding him, at least you can start with this name.' He handed him a sheet of paper that he had retrieved from his breast pocket. On it was scribbled in Peter's unique scrawl: 'Jazzy Networks.'

'Where did you get this from?' Dele asked.

'When you create a file, the computer you first created it on always leaves its mark on it,' he said and walked away quickly, in a self-possessed manner.

Dele shook his head. He tried the GSM number again. It just kept on ringing. Then he went to the office and retrieved the file. Ignatius's address was a cyber café, but it was not Jazzy Networks. He strongly suspected that it was a fake address but he noted it down. He then called his friend in the police, gave him the phone number and asked him to put out an alert for Ignatius. He also gave him the phone number. The reason: fraud. He then took the sheet of paper where he had written the address, got into his car and went out in search of Ignatius. Time was of the essence.

*

Ignatius went to the police station to report that his phone had been stolen. With no money in his pocket, he reluctantly had to go and see one of his old cleaner friends to bail him out of the embarrassing situation. This guy worked in a bank. Ignatius hated banks. He hated the situation he was in even more. After explaining his embarrassing situation, Ignatius had got enough money to get back home, with a bit of change to spare. He had used that to call his number several times but he had not gotten through. The only time he had, it rang for quite a while before the thief picked up the phone and told him to bring 15,000 naira to collect his phone. He was complaining about the sum when the connection had died. When he tried again, the phone just kept on ringing. He must have annoyed the thief. So he had decided to report to the police in order to reclaim his line. There was a lot of bantering in a corner of the station between some of the officers and the people in the small cell at the back. A sign which read 'Bail is Free' hung boldly, but loosely, over the counter. There were two persons behind the counter looking dejected. A policewoman stood there, like a shopkeeper.

'I came to report that my phone was stolen.'

'Won't you greet me first?' she countered acidly, a sneer on her face.

'Sorry, good morning ma'am. I am Ignatius Imodibo, my phone was stolen this morning and I need a police statement to be able to retrieve it.'

What did you say was your name?'

'Ignatius Imodibo.'

'Do you live at number 2 Atunrase Street?'

'Yes,' he replied, surprised.

'Mike, Joe, this is the man we have been looking for!' she screamed.

At this, two of the policemen at the corner of the room, swooped on him, knocking him down. Before he knew what was happening, he was behind the counter. He wasn't told his offence. His accuser would soon be at the station. Then, he would know.

*

Peter stared at the screen. Even though he now had some information about the owner of the program, he wasn't sure he could guess the password correctly since programmers tended to be eccentric about such things. The more complicated a problem seems, the simpler the solution. He decided to give it a go. He typed god: Incorrect Password. jesus: Incorrect. money: Incorrect. mom, portal, yes, no, passmark, great: all Incorrect. He stopped to think. What did Ignatius have written on the CD case? He typed payday:

Incorrect Password. He typed the words backwards: yadyap. The screen blinked. He was in. All of a sudden, the computer started booting. He sighed in relief. Now that the computer had started, he intended to find out what the cause of the problem was. Ignatius must be a dumb programmer, he thought. Imagine him writing the password on the case of the CD. He ran the program again. Everything seemed to be normal again. He then decided to see if he could view the source codes, the codes that ran the program. He could view them. He was surprised that someone who did something as good as this could allow his source codes to be viewed. This meant that anyone could pirate it. Anyway, what would you expect from an amateur, he thought. As he browsed through the codes, a thought descended upon him. Why not copy the codes out, polish one or two things, and then sell it to the company and other people who needed such a solution? He could think of several users already. And they would pay highly to have this, or even a lesser version of what he had now. He started copying them to his hard disk. In a short while, he was through.

*

Dele went with a driver and one of the office boys whose name was Andrew. Their first port of call was to be the address in the file. It was called Genesis Networks, somewhere in Aguda, Surulere. He dreaded the traffic that he had to go through in order to get from the Island to Surulere. It seemed so paradoxical. Places in Lagos were close, yet so far. If only he could get through to the phone number, things would be a lot easier. He kept on trying the number as they moved. When they were descending Carter Bridge to get to Surulere someone finally picked up the phone.

'Hello?'

'Hello.'

Dele sat bolt upright in his seat, excited.

'Is that Mr Ignatius Imodibo?'

'No.'

'Please can I speak to him, if he is anywhere near there? I am calling from Octan & Phillips. It is very urgent.'

The recipient hung up.

Dele redialed, furiously. It rang and rang with no answer. He thought of what Mr Phillips would expect of him. He had drummed the exigency of getting the systems running into his head. Ignatius would not mind some consideration. After all, he was calling all the shots now. He now decided to send a text message: we are ready to pay you some money if you respond.

No response.

'Where do we go from here?' the driver asked. They were in Aguda now. They decided to stop and hire a taxi that knew the area better, in order to reach the address of Genesis Networks. They meandered through the streets of Aguda for about twenty minutes before they finally got to the place. It was a non-descript one-storey building, with a faded sign in front of it. Through the windows, one could clearly see it was a low-level cyber café. After paying the driver, he walked into the building with the caution of an alien from space. There was a young lady selling log-on time near the entrance. A young fellow was standing at the counter next to her, apparently chatting her up. Dele walked up to the lady and asked to see the manager. The young fellow turned towards him.

'Why do you want to see him?' the young man asked.

Dele shrugged and then said, 'I am looking for one Ignatius Imodibo that works here.'

'Ah! Ignatius? He used to work here. He left about four months ago. He was a very quiet fellow. Why do you want to see him?'

'I have a message from someone he did business for. He recommended him highly, that is why I am here. Do you know how I can reach him? It is urgent.'

'Why don't you call him?'

'There seems to be a problem with his phone. I have been trying all day. Do you know where he lives or where he works?'

The boy looked at the lady. They looked up in thought. After a while, the girl ventured,' I think you should ask Yisa. If anyone knows how to reach him, Yisa is the man. They were quite close.'

The young man disappeared through a door in the corner of the hall, ostensibly to call Yisa. After a while, a wiry, dark boy beaming from ear to ear appeared.

'Good day sir, I understand that you are looking for Ignatius.' The smile on his face seemed to be permanent.

Dele nodded.

'Well, he works at Jazzy Networks in Idimu, near his house. I have never gone there but I understand it is very popular. Maybe it is the only cyber café they have in that area. You know those places are like villages, being in the outskirts of Lagos…'

'Is that all you know?' Dele cut him short.

'Well, yes, I normally reach him by phone although he has not called me in a while. I haven't called him in a while either, you know how bad these networks can be at times just to call someone next to you…'

'Well, thank you very much.' The lady at the counter and the other young man giggled as Yisa was cut short again. 'I will try to locate him at Idimu, then.'

As he stepped out of the building, his phone started ringing. It was Ignatius's number.

'So you are ready to bring the 15,000 naira I told you to bring now eh?'

Dele was confused. He hadn't discussed any money with the fellow on the phone. Anyway, the fee seemed to be paltry compared to the havoc he had caused in the office.

'There is a dustbin at the side of First Bank, Marina, put the money in a black nylon bag there. I will call you on how to get your phone back.'

So his phone had been stolen. There was no point haggling with a phone thief. He hung up. As soon as he put the phone in his pocket, it started ringing again. He looked at the number. This one was Mr Phillips. He would be asking for results now. It was already three o'clock. He hesitated before answering the call.

'Dele, have you found him?'

'I am on my way to his house now sir" he lied.

'Get him fast. The Ministry of Works is on my neck concerning the projects we should have delivered last week. Have you informed the police yet?'

'Yes sir.'

'Well, I will do so again. Call me as soon as you catch him.' The line went dead.

Dele walked towards the car, confused. He hissed. He hated the pressure that his boss usually put on him.

'*Oga*, where do we go from here?' the driver asked.

'Andrew,' he called the office hand, 'I want you to take a taxi to the Island, get an IOU of 15,000 naira from the office and get the phone from this thief. I will call the police to give you one of their men to follow you. I don't know what kind of people you may meet.'

The young man nodded.

'Driver, we are going to Idimu.'

*

Ignatius sat in a corner behind the counter with a sullen look on his face. He had been there for about three hours now. He hadn't been beaten but he had received a few kicks from criminals who were being led behind bars. A sadistic policeman had also slapped him for obstructing him. What traumatised him the most were the howls he heard in the cells behind him. He knew the cells would be his fate if some help did not come fast. But where was his accuser anyway? They said that they'd sent someone to fetch him; still, no response. He looked at the decrepit notice again: bail is free. It would have been laughable if he didn't need it now. But, of course, it wasn't true. People were all over the place haggling for their freedom with the police who didn't have time for a penniless nobody like him. He needed someone from the outside to help him. He decided to walk up to the policewoman at the counter and ask her to get someone for him – he needed to contact his neighbour! Even though he didn't talk with them much, they couldn't abandon him now, if only out of good neighbourliness.

As he rose and walked towards her, he looked at the world beyond the counter. There were two young girls talking to a policeman who was nodding his head in understanding as they talked. One of them looked familiar, like someone he knew, though her back was facing him. Then, she turned. Even in the dim light, he could still not mistake that face, even after all these years.

'Cordelia!' he shouted.

'Ignatius!' she called, and ran towards him, stopped by the counter barrier.

'What are you doing in Lagos? How did you find me here?'

'Papa Abel told me how to get to your house. When I got there and asked for you, the people in the compound said they didn't know you. I had almost given up hope until a small boy called me and told me that the police was looking for you. He told me how to get here.'

'Is the boy dark with three tribal marks on each cheek?'

'Yes.'

'That's Moruf. He's my friend.'

'What did you do?'

'I don't know. I came here to report that my phone had been stolen and they arrested me. But how did Moruf know I was here? I hadn't sent any message to the compound yet. By the way, what *are* you doing in Lagos?'

'Mama is seriously sick. She has been admitted to hospital and has to have an operation. They sent me to Lagos to tell you.'

'What kind of operation is it?'

'It has something to do with the first signs of cancer. They said that to remove the tumours, they will need to do an operation. But it would be better that they fly her abroad. She is still in intensive care. Uncle Sunday has only managed part of that hospital bill so far. I think they estimated, for everything, 200,000 naira.'

'My God! 200,000 naira! If I had 2,000 naira I wouldn't still be in here.'

By then, tears were now rolling down Cordelia's cheeks.

'I still have about 500 naira here. Let me see if I can talk to the police to get you out.'

As she turned towards the policewoman on the other side of the counter, the lady started coming towards them in haste.

'Aha! This man said you stole 10,000 naira from his house this morning. Where did you keep it?'

She pointed at a bespectacled short man in a dirty flowing *agbada* whom Ignatius recognised as one of his co-tenants, Mr Lasaki. He had had several brushes with the man concerning the payment of electricity bills, as they always failed to reach an equitable sharing formula every time the collective bill came. The man also hated him because he claimed that Ignatius never accorded him the due respect that his age demanded. Now this! The man had finally decided to take his grievances to the police station.

'Yes, yes, that's him. Yesterday, I brought back some money given to me as advance payment to buy some batteries. I charge batteries for a living. This morning I woke up at 6.30 am and the money was gone. I started asking people in the compound and they said that they didn't take it. This man went out before 5 o'clock with my money. Has he confessed?'

'Mr Lasaki, I have never entered your house in all my life. How could I enter and steal your money now?' Ignatius retorted.

'That doesn't mean anything. One can enter a house for the first time and steal something,' the policewoman added.

Suddenly, one of the other policemen beckoned the policewoman to come to the entrance of the police station. She dashed down. Ignatius stared at them confounded. Then he gave Cordelia and Mr Lasaki questioning looks. Cordelia stared back and Mr Lasaki looked away. Soon enough, the two police officers walked back in with a middle aged man. He was decked in a dark blue suit, a white shirt, a red tie and black shoes. He exuded a certain level of affluence that made one wonder what he would be looking for in a dingy place like the station. The group walked towards Ignatius, stopping some distance in front of the counter.

'Are you Ignatius Imodibo?' the man asked.

Ignatius stared, confused, then slowly nodded. 'Yes.'

'My name is Dele Durojaiye. I am from Octan & Phillips, concerning the program you wrote for us.'

'Proteus Pro? It's a portal, not a program.'

Cordelia and Mr Lasaki were the ones who now looked bewildered.

'Well, it has crashed our network and we can't access any of our systems. So I was sent to find you to fix it.'

'So it worked!' Ignatius exclaimed, showing some excitement for the first time. 'Well, you can see my condition. I will have to get out of here first before we can talk.'

'Why are you being detained?'

'This man,' he said, pointing derisively at Mr Lasaki, 'claims I stole his money: 10,000 naira.'

'Yes, yes, you stole my money!' Mr Lasaki shouted, suddenly invigorated.

'So if I give you 10,000 naira, you will let this man out of this cell?' Dele asked.

'Yes, now!' the police officers chorused.

Dele flipped out his wallet and counted the money out quickly, holding it out to them. Mr Lasaki lunged at it but Cordelia blocked him. 'Don't give him, he is lying, he is a thief!' Mr Lasaki pushed her away and grabbed the money. The police officers blocked his retreat.

'Ah, *oga*, anything for us?' the policeman asked for his own kickback. It wasn't clear if he expected to get it from Mr Lasaki or from Dele. Dele counted out five two-hundreds and handed them to the police.

'Now, can we go?'

It wasn't really a question because he started walking away before they replied. Ignatius followed behind him, with Cordelia walking beside him.

'Thank you sir, God bless you sir, may you live long sir,' she prayed as she walked beside him. The words seemed inadequate. He was like an angel from God. When they got next to his car, Dele suddenly asked: 'Is your sister going back with us? She *is* your sister?'

'Yes she is and I think she should come with us. I don't want her anywhere near those vultures who call themselves my neighbours. Her name is Cordelia. Cordelia meet Mr … er…'

'Mr Durojaiye, I work for Octan & Phillips, a consulting firm that Ignatius, em … works for.'

Cordelia turned to Ignatius, confused.

'No, I just did a small contract with them and they haven't paid me for it yet.'

'I spoke to Mr Phillips once we had confirmed you were in this station. Anyway, he told us to bring you to his office to talk, as soon as we got you out. Do you want to speak with him before we go?' He pulled out a handset from his pocket. Ignatius took the phone recognising it at once. It was his phone.

'How did you find it? How did you find me?'

Dele didn't respond immediately. He only waved them into the car. Cordelia sat on the passenger's seat while Ignatius and Dele sat at the back.

'It was your friend at Jazzy Networks, Yisa, that led us to your house: a real chatterbox.'

'How did you know I worked for Jazzy Networks? I just worked there for a month.'

'I think only Peter can answer that. He said something about a program leaving tracks of where it was made, something like that.' Ignatius nodded his head in understanding.

'Now, why did you decide to wreck our office with your program? I think it was highly irresponsible. If not for Mr Phillips, I would have let you spend a night or two in that cell to teach you a lesson.'

'I won't say I am sorry. I am proud that it worked, so well that you had to overcome all the obstacles to find me. Thank you. I thought that you would just have to call me… But how did you get my phone back?'

Dele eyed him, annoyed. 'What do you think? We simply contacted the guy and paid for the phone back. Again, Mr Phillips's prerogative, not mine.'

'Well, maybe I will save all the thanks for him.'

'Thank you sir,' Cordelia chipped in.

By this time, they were on the bridge to the Island. Most commuters were going out of the Island. As they were going in, it was smooth sailing. It was seven o'clock. There was silence till they reached the Island. As they descended the bridge, the Island shone with a thousand lights of different colours, beckoning them to come. The buildings, which were beautiful in the day, looked magnificent at night. Mr Phillips called to confirm that they were on their way. Afterwards, silence descended upon the vehicle again. While Cordelia stared wide-eyed through the window, Ignatius had a short nap.

They soon got to the office building. Ignatius was nudged awake. They quickly shuffled out of the car and into the main building. By then, it was nine, with virtually no one left in the building. Two security men strolled around the compound. Ignatius only noticed lights in two offices, both on the uppermost floor. He imagined one of them belonged to his client.

'I think your sister should wait in the car, as we shouldn't be long.'

'No,' Ignatius protested, 'I want her to come with us. She didn't come here by accident. She has a role to play in this now.'

One of the security men rushed to open the main entrance but Dele waved him off, telling him not to worry as he opened the entrance door with his own key. They entered the dark and empty reception. Dele turned on the lights so they could find their way to the staircase. They walked up the stairs to the fifth floor. Mr Phillips's office was at the end of the corridor.

Ignatius mulled over the fact that he had been here almost twelve hours ago. Then, it had been all excitement, now he had mixed feelings, a deeper sense of purpose, even a bit of anger. Then, he was thinking about money for himself, now his family was involved, desperately. He stared at Cordelia, his lips becoming taut, a deep furrow forming on his brow. His face hardened as his will became resolute.

Dele opened the door to the office. Mr Phillips was seated like a demigod facing the door, his face hard. Peter stood in a corner of the room. He looked like a fowl beaten by the rain. It was clear that Mr Phillips must have given him a tongue-lashing, no doubt about that. He clenched his fists when he sighted Ignatius.

'Great Ignatius Imodibo! Why did you have to do this to us? We had an agreement and you decided to default it by running my company aground. Do you know that we couldn't do any work today? Do you know how much that has cost the company? I have a major contract as a consultant to the government worth millions of naira. We were seriously behind schedule and now you have almost killed it. We were meant to deliver a host of drawings tomorrow. I have been trying to get to the minister, in order to tell him that there may be a slight delay. Do you know what that means to my company, this country and to you? How do you think I get money to pay you if you sabotage my work like this? Now, get on that computer and undo what you have done.'

'And what if I don't?' Ignatius asked, defiant.

Mr Phillips virtually reeled back in shock. Few people talked to him like that, fewer still of Ignatius's age.

'What do you mean 'what if I don't'? Then you don't get paid and I will have you arrested. Maybe you should spend one or two nights in jail and then you'll come back to your senses.' Peter cringed in a corner.

'Well, I don't know the password to unlock it.'

Dele hissed.

'What do you mean you don't know the password?' Mr Phillips ranted.

'Well, the password changes every six hours. That was how it was set. I didn't create that. My friend did. The program is such that it prompts the owner's account balance through the internet. When the right amount of money is credited to that account, then it will open by itself. If not, then you will continue having the same problems and there is nothing you can do about it. If you send me to jail, your problem won't be solved. My sister here just came from the village to tell me that my dear mother is sick and needs to be sent abroad for an operation. The only way out is to pay up.'

'And how much is that?'

'The agreed sum, no more, no less.' Peter shook his head. This seemed like blackmail; but then again, it was the agreed sum.

'Why do you have to go through all this to get paid? Virtually close down my company, set this thing to your bank account: this is madness.' Mr Phillips now sounded quite subdued.

'Well, this thing has been dragging on for too long. I hated that and that made me lose any confidence in you. There are many people in this country who are highly skilled but are constantly being exploited by their employers. They pay them peanuts if they do pay at all, so those who want and are able to − like Mark − leave the country. I don't want to leave, at least not yet. This was simply to ensure that there would not be any further postponements. So I asked Mark to help me write the code for that.'

'We will pay by cheque first thing tomorrow morning but I want you to sign an undertaking that nothing of the sort will repeat itself again. If not, I will see that you get thrown into jail for a long time.'

'I have no problem with that,' Ignatius assured. 'There is one small thing. No one should try to copy the codes. The parts of the code that can't be viewed will crash the system it is copied to.'

Peter winced. His game was up. He'd been bested by a school drop-out! Luckily, no one noticed.

Mr Phillips brought out a sheet of paper and drafted a simple contract outlining all he had just said. Ignatius read through it and, satisfied, smiled. Cordelia smiled too.

Mr Phillips offered his hand. Ignatius grabbed it in a warm handshake. He couldn't believe that it would end so easily.

'You are a very shrewd young man. So what do you intend to do with the money, if I may ask?'

'Well, I wanted to go back to school with it but now that my mother is ill, most of it will probably go into that. I will go see her first thing tomorrow morning. I will look around for other people who are interested in my baby and make some money for myself.'

Mr Phillips nodded his head and smiled slightly.

'Although you didn't mention it, I guess I'll have to be under your custody till the program starts working well again?' Ignatius asked.

'Yes. I would rather you remain here. You can make yourself feel at home,' Mr Phillips said.

'It's fine with me, I don't even have a place to spend the night,'

After a while, Peter asked to take his leave. Mr Phillips waved him off. Ignatius walked him to the door, a grin on his face.

'So you've managed to get your money from Mr Phillips,' Peter whispered.

'Thank you for the advice. I couldn't have done it without you, you know,' Ignatius replied.

'Oh, what I told you in the waiting room: always have cards left to play?'

'Yes.'

'Hope to see you around some other time.'

'The pleasure is mine.'

Ignatius smiled as he closed the door behind Peter. He turned to face Mr Phillips with a deadpan expression on his face.

The day was over.

ROAD RAGE
Rotimi Ogunjobi

'Good morning Musa,' said the Mercedes.

Musa struggled with himself to remain unperturbed. Instead he gave the fading red car a civil nod which was barely perceptible to anyone who might have been watching. The car grinned back with metallic malice.

'Come on man, I'm not going to eat you,' the Mercedes encouraged. But Musa was not quite convinced. Indeed, he expected the car to do something quite in line with his fearful expectations, like leaping off the ground and biting his arm off.

Monster Motor Mauls Man.

Great alliterative headline that would make for any newspaper in the world any day, he thought to himself.

Musa had a constant morning departure ritual before leaving for work, and it was the kind patently created for television. He kisses his wife Zainab, kisses his two daughters, picks up his briefcase and goes off to work. Zainab and his four-year-old twin daughters are in the front porch of the house waving and cheering. There is no going back on this at all. What would the children say to their friends: you think your dad is weird? Mine is scared that his car is going to eat him.

The red Mercedes laughed wickedly.

In panic, a fleeting thought to take a taxi instead occurred to Musa.

'And don't start getting the idea again of going off without me, you can't afford a taxi you know?' the car reminded.

'No I can't,' Musa agreed.

'You want to go to work in a *Molue* instead then?'

'Of course not, those contraptions are not fit for human beings,' Musa was horrified.

'Okay, get all that into your skull and let's roll. And remember anyway that you have your important client to visit tonight. Tonight is dinner with Sam Ikumejakako and if it rains you'll probably not find a taxi to take you there, or, worse still, you will arrive at the golf club soaked, which wouldn't do your company, or your client, proud at all.'

'Oh yes, I know,' Musa said tiredly as he unlocked the door of the car. Every morning he secretly hoped that the car would not start, but it always did. It was not that he hated the car so much; because he was indeed also afraid of the consequences of it not starting in the morning. He definitely could not afford to go to work ten miles away in a taxi every morning, and going by bus was even more unthinkable. The car had him in a spiritual arm-lock. And apart from quickly becoming a financial liability with its nascent drink and smoke problem, the car had been of late, leading him to do a lot of funny mathematics – and *this* was a lot more serious.

Musa took a deep breath and composed himself as he turned the ignition. The car started as expected and Musa sighed resignedly. What to do then? Self-hypnosis: relax, say to yourself I am relaxed, I am cool, I am calm, and everything is okay. But we know that Musa is not okay, right?

'Have you taken your tranks today... tranks today... tranks today...' the car's tired engine tapped out a tiresome tune.

'Shut up', Musa asserted himself to Red Mercedes.

He suddenly realised that the children and Zainab were looking at him quite anxiously. He contrived a smile, waved cheerfully and slowly eased the car out of the yard into the street.

'Tranks today...tranks today...' Red Mercedes persisted.

'Hush now, you stupid lump of German junk', Musa pleaded.

'I thought to give you a good copy for a road etiquette campaign', the Mercedes sounded hurt. '*Have you taken your tranquillisers today?*'

'Don't tell me about a copy. I am the advertising guy remember? And you, my friend, are destined for the junkyard, so, again, I say shut up!'

The Mercedes complied and sulked, 'Tranks today... tranks today...' it muttered.

Musa allowed himself to relax into the soft seat. He reached into his briefcase and took out a notepad and a ballpoint pen. Laying both lovingly on the car seat beside him, he drove his car into the traffic on the main road. The vibration of the tired engine traveled through the steering wheel and into his hands. It had a somewhat thrilling effect. Musa allowed the vibration to ripple through his arms and to his body and it was an almost sexual feeling. He stepped on the throttle pedal and the car vibrated harder. An image of a sexy girl riding a big bike lingered deliciously on his mind for a long moment.

'Thinking about girls Musa?' the Mercedes whispered conspiratorially. 'Now you know why those young chicks like to ride on motor cycle taxis.'

Musa refused to answer; he did, in fact, feel somewhat embarrassed.

'There is this theory that a man who loves his car so very much is not likely to be much in love with his wife, except probably if she were also aerodynamically styled and wore a lot of shiny paint,' Red Mercedes persisted.

'Stupid cliché,' Musa snorted.

'I also learnt that a woman who is obsessed with her car often does not have a steerable husband.'

'You must have been drinking the wrong kind of petrol. I sure hope for your sake that cars don't get brain rot,' Musa said wickedly.

'You don't believe in clichés, eh? I'm going to tell you something Musa baby; you mess with not believing clichés and you mess with not having a job anymore. That's what advertising is all about isn't it? You mess with cliché baby and you'll have to sell me off to be able to feed your family, okay?' Red Mercedes advised. Musa suppressed his happiness at this suggestion.

'Give me a break you metal geek,' he pleaded

'Hey, dig this Musa: Man + beautiful car = beautiful girlfriend. Okay? Hey, dig this: Woman + Lovely car = many excited male admirers. Right? Hey, dig this: good copy Musa baby!' The car was definitely in high spirits as it sped along.

Musa couldn't suppress the laughter. It was quite true, of course. But somehow the way the crazy car had said it appeared to suggest that a woman was like a mere accessory to a car? Musa was a thinking man and that was what he thought. His other thinking was also that since the purveyors and the consumers appear to fancy this association, why spoil the fun. There were some basic issues that you questioned at the risk of your career.

Musa switched on the radio for the morning news, out of habit actually. He turned up the volume high enough to forestall any interference from the pesky car. Like most people, Musa always had the feeling that the day had not properly begun without the presence of the morning news. Listening to the news did different things for different people. Primarily, it assured that the world was still on its crazy course which, for the schizophrenic and permanent pessimist, meant that wringing the hands and lamenting in response to the hopelessness of it all was a normal, acceptable and quite justifiable social behaviour. For the conceited ones, it was extra fuel of assurance and vanity that, in spite of the whole global mess, you were still within yourself a serene oasis amidst the parched desert – *in compos mentis*, which was why the world kept on its crazy course. Again today Musa was pleased not to be dead or constipated with hopelessness.

At the next junction a traffic policeman was idly standing by the roadside with a baseball bat in hand and a real lunatic with long, brown, tangled hair and tattered clothes was directing the traffic. Yet, the traffic was somehow still not moving.

'You see that? Some fool is probably sitting there in his car and counting his fingers,' Musa complained to Red Mercedes, 'This can only happen in Lagos, you know.'

Musa thrust his head out of the window and reminded the errant driver, whoever he was, to go visit the rest of his family in the asylum. Having fulfilled his civic obligation he felt that he had no other choice than to wait. In the interim, he decided to examine a theory which had suddenly presented itself fiercely in his mind:

$$A = \bigcup_{1}^{m} \int_{-\infty}^{\infty} f(P)$$

[Where P represents possession and A aggression.]

That was what Musa wrote in his notepad whilst waiting for the traffic to flow again. He looked at what he had written and nodded proudly.

'Not bad for a guy who had flunked O-level mathematics, eh,' he told Red Mercedes. However, he noted that the theorem clearly did not explain whether the relationship applied equally to drivers as well as pedestrians, but that would be trashed out within a few moments, right?

He found himself thinking about the important dinner engagement for later in the day with Sam Ikumejakako.

'You smashed the ass of his new car you careless crank,' Red Mercedes interrupted his thought.

'No I did not, you did,' Musa replied, 'And anyway it was him that broke suddenly.'

'Even if he did brake suddenly you were at fault, that's what the law says.'

Indeed that was the way the argument had gone on that particular day.

'To hell with the law, the world could do with a lot less maniacs like you,' Musa had raved at the quite bemused Ikumejakako standing quietly beside his injured sky blue Mercedes convertible, latest model.

Nevertheless, they had exchanged insurance details and Musa had conceded a half-hearted undertaking to repair the damaged rear fender of Ikumejakako's car.

'Idiot,' he had muttered as he went away.

In retrospect, he would confess that his anger had actually been directed at the expensive car, which he had no hope of being able to afford, rather than at its owner. And so, quite sorry for his behaviour, Musa had called Ikumejakako a couple of hours later to apologise.

'All is forgiven,' Ikumejakako had replied, and on learning that Musa was an advertising executive, he had invited him to a dinner meeting for later that day at the golf club. Things had gone marvelously well between them since then. Ikumejakako had turned out to be owner of a large merchandising company, and he was pleased to engage Musa's company to move his many products along in the market. This was how Musa netted for his employers the largest account that they had ever signed, together with the promise of a big bonus at the end of the year and, possibly, of a promotion and maybe even a company car.

Musa was tugged back to thinking about the relationship between cars and their owners. As everyone in the world knows, a car is a *quantity*, it being the summation of the owner's self worth. A car projects the intensity of the need of the owner for attention or recognition. Thus:

$$I = \phi(-c)$$

Which implies that the self-worth suggested by the car is directly proportionate to the quantity of idiocy that is likely to be exhibited by the subject owner.

'What nonsense to suggest that idiocy is a functional derivative of the possession of an automobile,' Red Mercedes sounded disgusted.

'There are a lot more idiots who cannot even afford to buy a car horn and spend their lives scrambling to get on a crammed bus, to jobs which barely paid enough to cover the bus fare.'

'Must you have an answer to everything I think? Get out of my head!' Musa protested.

'I'm trying. You think I like to be inside there?' Red Mercedes said stiffly.

Mercifully, the queue began once again to move. It gave him a fresh surge of inspiration and new insights to the work at hand. He always found it a lot easier to create better copy while driving.

'Something Extraordinary Is About To Happen…. Nothing!

How is that as caption for the visual of a rock being hurled at a sheet of armored glass?' He gleefully asked Red Mercedes.

'Go Ahead. Take Your Best Shot. Try and imagine that one with a terrorist carrying a machine gun. Eh, eh,' he laughed.

Musa loved his job. His only problem was the people with worthless wares seeking some magic words and pictures to make others take out their wallets and spend. But then, business is not about moralizing, it is about getting fed, getting paid, and getting rich. The wise ones do the *getting*. There were indeed some facts of life, which one needed always face, chief of which is that it takes both the wise guys and the fools to move the world along. Musa was glad that he didn't belong in the latter camp.

Okay, advertising may not look quite all glamour anymore, especially after you'd seen the movie *Crazy People*, in which a bunch of people from a mental hospital get themselves organised and consulted by Big Business to churn out drop-dead advertisement that actually make products sell… like mad. But it was the only life that Musa knew, and it was the only job he felt suited for. Pity it didn't pay much and his family's needs were increasing fast. The twins would soon need to start school. Zainab would soon need her own car to take the twins to school and to bring them back home. But as things were, he was struggling fiercely with his finances and, as Zainab didn't work, they had to learn to survive on his pay packet.

'Let Us Teach Your Men How To Screw!' Musa hooted. 'I bet that would be a great attention-grabber for the training workshop those Labour Union guys are organising for industrial artisans.'

We Like Dirty Stories. He considered that idea for a detergent manufacturer.

It Is Not The Size, It Is The Satisfaction. Now, shouldn't that settle the soft drink market war once and for all?

A Lexus four-wheeler rolled to a stop beside his car.

Precious Metal, Musa instinctively thought. However, he was suddenly jolted to the reality that he was, again, not moving.

'Can you believe this? Some idiot probably fell asleep at the wheel and cracked his head on the windscreen,' he complained to Red Mercedes. 'Do you think he's dead?'

'It's a traffic light,' Red Mercedes told him.

'Hey, if I needed your opinion, I would have asked, okay?' Musa snapped, 'One could spend an entire lifetime waiting on the road because the whole world is full of nincompoops.'

He became again aware that the chauffeured owner of the Lexus was staring at him.

'Why are you looking at me like that?' Musa angrily demanded.

As Musa, and indeed everyone in the world knew people only looked at you to compare cars – especially the physical condition, and value. They looked at you to evaluate your *quantity*.

'His damned Lexus doesn't make him any better than anyone else on the road, does it?' he said for the benefit of the amused spectator. 'Okay he's probably got several other cars, but try riding two cars at the same time mister and see how big a fool you're going to look.'

To take his mind off the present irritation, Musa busied himself with more productive cerebration:

$$\sum_{1}^{n} C = S$$

Which was to say that the level of sanity is definitely influenced by the number of cars possessed by a person. Musa shook his head. He was not satisfied with that. More accurately:

$$S = Y(a)\sigma\sqrt{\pi a}$$

[Where S = sanity.]

But this would truly be an inverse quadratic function in which S must assume its highest value as the value of car variable (a) tends to zero.

'Heavy scene,' cackled Red Mercedes, 'Hey Musa, your mother's going to be very proud of you. Look this way everybody, my son is a roadside psychiatrist. My Musa is a distinguished maniac.'

All around, tempers were rising high. The noise of blaring horns and cursing people filled the air. Home is the only place where you were guaranteed to find sanity, Musa thought ruefully. Pity you can't take your home along with you when you go out, no matter how lovely it is. Outside the home, your car is the ambassador of your family and, as far as he knew, people were often more interested in the state of health of your car, than that of your children. And when you have a really bashed up car, people can immediately see how much your entire family is suffering, the car being a bona fide and prime representative of you all in terms of physical well-being.

The traffic was again in motion. The radio was blasting out loud rap music.

'Do you like this?' Musa asked Red Mercedes

'It's cool.'

'I thought you would say that. It's also cool to a whole generation of half-wits.'

'Hey, chill man,' Red Mercedes frostily replied.

'Chill? You are twenty years old, you metal misery. And in my time, and also yours, it was okay to be cool, meaning you were okay with the world and, especially, with yourself. *Mens sana in corpore sano*, right? Chill was what you did, or, more correctly, what they did to you when you were dead and waiting to be buried. Okay?'

'It's cool man. Don't burst a vein.'

'That's right, only you've got to watch out you don't say cool anymore because people sort of begin to think that you are into doing drugs, or, worse, an old guy trying to be cool, which is not a really cool feeling at all.'

'Okay you are getting old, is that easier to live with?' Red Mercedes asked.

Angrily, Musa stepped on the throttle pedal. The car wound

dangerously through the gaps in the traffic.

Musa put the Red Mercedes neck-to-neck in a race with an equally affected driver. He sent a group of crossing school children scampering for dear life, and nearly crippled a few of them.

'Can you keep up?' Musa asked Red Mercedes.

'Are you kidding?' Red Mercedes replied.

Thus, they embarked together on a convoluted mathematical odyssey. Inspired calculations thoroughly engulfed his mind, flowing out of his mouth, nostrils, ears… twirling around him like candy floss. As he sped along, he created a dozen new theorems which harnessed all the mysteries of velocity, payload, fuel flow rate, engine efficiency and some other parameters for which no name yet existed. Damn, I am a genius, Musa thought. He made an emphatic mental note to get himself a tape recorder or one of those computer gadgets to record all this stuff.

Musa was again forced to stop suddenly. A woman in a custard yellow Toyota Something was finding it difficult to make a turning quickly enough. Musa advised her to tell her husband to get a real job so that she could afford a chauffeur.

The woman in the Toyota advised Musa to change his doctor for a vet.

Musa was interested to know how much she paid to get her driving license.

She told Musa how sure she was that whatever he had smoked for breakfast that morning was certainly stronger than tobacco.

Musa informed her that he indeed had this very morning breakfasted with her daddy.

Exasperated, the woman had lamented that anyone could have mistaken Musa for a gentleman, and Musa was flummoxed.

'Did you hear that?' He asked Red Mercedes. 'Stupid bitch says I am not a gentleman. Tell me, how does she know? It takes a true lady to know a true gentleman, doesn't it?'

'Hey, take it easy man,' Red Mercedes cajoled.

'Take it easy my ass,' Musa fumed, 'A lousy two-point turning on a thirty foot wide road! Surely any idiot should be able to do that. Stupid… stupid… stupid… Her husband must have won her in a lottery, and having never won anything before in his whole life, the idiot must have decided against common sense to keep her.'

So Musa, the gentle husband and loving father, sideswiped the woman's custard yellow Toyota Something with his red Mercedes, ripped off her rear fender, and sped away leaving behind a thick exhaust of environmentalist-unfriendly black smoke and a flurry of very colourful curses.

'Dynoooomite,' the Mercedes purred with pure pleasure. Musa slapped his forehead merrily.

'Did you see the look on the bitch's face?' he asked Red Mercedes. 'She thought I was going to kill her,' Musa slipped on his dark glasses. The noisy unintelligible rap music was beginning to initiate a headache now. He fed a cassette into the tape slot; a rich, mellow jazzy tune rumbled out from the car's heavy one-thousand-watt speakers.

'Ladies and gentlemen, here is Roger Miller's voice singing "King of The Road", number one on the world chart, May 13, 1965. Now this is music!' Musa announced and he sang along:

No phone, no pool, no pets
I ain't got no cigarettes...

Musa had a cigarette. And he lit it.

FRAGILE
Uchechukwu Peter Umezurike

Early Nineties

Ijeoma and I did not get along as friends. I was the bookish, skirt-and-blouse type. She was the carefree, miniskirt-or-jeans girl. I wore thick glasses that gave me the unexciting looks of a bore. I disliked putting them on, but without those glasses, I would only grope around because of myopia. Ijeoma had brown eyes that twinkled when she smiled.

She walks in beauty, like the night
of cloudless climes and starry skies

I was ordinary-looking, like a village girl. Sometimes, I had to put on shorts to pad out my buttocks, for a well-rounded effect. Ijeoma had the right curves for skin-tight wear. Shapely hips, plump backside, slim waist. She was stunning in jeans or tights and men used to ogle at her even whilst in the presence of their girlfriends. Every male student strove to hang out with her. Every female student struggled to be her friend. She was always in the midst of both sexes: radiant.

Girls spent months practising for the annual Campus Queen pageant. Ijeoma won the crown, without straining a muscle. She often behaved meekly. But how could she? Was it possible? Doesn't beauty and pride walk hand-in-hand? Didn't I have four eyes? One afternoon Ugomma and I were eating at the refectory. I asked her if she had noticed anything about Miss Peacock. I personally referred to Ijeoma as Miss Peacock.

'Like what?' Ugomma asked. She was my reading partner, a bibliophile.

'I feel something is not quite right with her,' I said.

'You're funny, Nky. Nothing is wrong with Ijeoma.'

'You don't feel it?'

'Christ! I feel you don't really fancy her style,' she spoke a bit too loudly.

The other students looked at us.

'There is something strange…I think she's…' I said after a while.

Ijeoma sat next to me during lectures. Occasionally, though. We barely spoke. We ignored each other like two girls bearing malice. I would not speak to her, for all I cared. I was sure Ijeoma was not what she seemed to be. I could almost see it, that spurious thing in her twinkling eyes and graceful gait. Then, she suddenly struck me as a mermaid.

Do not play
With the Daughter of the Sea

Ijeoma began grinning at me whenever we met in class. I scarcely grinned back, because I perceived she was making fun of me in a secret way. Before then, she and Anne would stare at me and whisper to each other whenever they sighted me. Often she would ask, 'Did you buy that hand-out? Were you in the lecture? Did they sign the attendance register? I heard we are taking a test. When?'

I didn't consider it wise to get on with her, so I answered her enquiries with the crisp tact a politician adopts in replying to a journalist. Have you heard of a fabled snake that befriends its prey before it releases its venom? Still, students warmed to Ijeoma easily, as if she gave out the most sought-after bursary allowance. I fumed inwardly as they fought to gain her attention and I squirmed when the lousy males lavished her with more compliments than was normal. She made me feel as if I were the ugliest girl on campus! And so, waiting for lectures became unbearable. I started avoiding lectures. Why steam away in a class of fulsome fools when I could read in the library?

Later, with inch-thick specs,
Evil was just my lark.

Lying on my bed at night, I would wonder how a student could be so fortunate. I was familiar with tales of how girls from the 'Spirit

World' lived among humans. They drank life to the lees and seldom lacked anything. Ijeoma wasn't intelligent as such. How come she didn't flunk a course? Quite often, before I slept, I did wish I would wake up and hear something bad had befallen her. Wouldn't it be interesting if she were raped by some cult members? She would be caricatured on the campus bulletin board as a cringing bitch. What would be left of her dignity?

One early morning I woke to the sound of merry 'Girls ayes!' I jumped down from my bunk bed. I didn't even think it might have been a student strike, a burglar, or a fire that had burst out from a student's cooker in the hostel. Some girls were crying out, stamping their feet. I thought what I had wished for Ijeoma had come true!

The toxin of Jealousy
Burns the heart with fervour

My stomach tightened. What greeted my ears was definitely not true! No, no! It must be some outrageous rumour. Weeks later, her friends hosted a party for her in the lounge of the female hostel. She would relocate to South Africa and take up a full-time modeling contract. It was as if she had pushed me into a stinking gutter and all the other students were mocking me. She was a mermaid, I was now convinced. That night I slept off campus, in town, with a friend. I almost smashed my glasses against the wall of her room as I lay in bed, fever heating up my head. Soon after, Ijeoma went abroad. Good riddance, I said. Thankfully enough, my results did not drop. I'd begun obtaining very high grades. I became one of the top three students in my class. On few occasions, my name was announced: the only student with the highest score for a particular course.

And my name blew
Like a horn
Among the Payira

I soon grew to a personality among my course-mates. In class and during exams, boys and girls struggled to sit beside me. My jotter and jottings became sought-after, like gems.

Nky, you are brilliant!
That's Nky, the girl...
Who? Oh, she's the one?
Yes, she is the brightest in her class.

Miss Peacock was no more. I had seized her spot-light. I was not shaped for beauty but I was singled out for brilliance. Like her, I basked in popularity, but I was naturally unassuming. I did not want to be seen as an arrogant person. And, unlike her, I was esteemed, an academic award-winner.

*

Late Nineties
It was by sheer happenstance that we met again. One sunny noon, I boarded an *inaga* to the market, when another cyclist swished off a narrow road onto Zander Street.

Constantly risking absurdity and death
Whenever he performs

The cyclist was singing like a sot as he approached us. He shot out a hand and waved it vigorously, like a politician. Bystanders looked at him: some fellow cyclists cheered him on, others sneered. It was a stupid act, but he seemed thrilled. A wide pothole lay on the road yawning like the jaws of a shark. I knew the cyclist wouldn't see the pothole in time. He dodged it, deftly though.
A child ran across the road. Onlookers cried out. But the cyclist, trying to avoid spilling innocent blood, veered off his lane onto ours. Brakes squealed like wounded pigs. Tires screeched as both motorcycles went into a skid. Tiny sparks flew off the roughly tarred road. I was thrown off the motorcycle before I could scream. I fell on my chest. Spots of black and white, like moths, flickered before me, as if I were underwater. I squeezed my eyes shut but I was spiraling down a dark, dark hole. Afterwards, my eyes opened. I was sitting on the ground, legs spread-out, too dazed to stand, the sculpture of a sorrowing widow.
Strange voices rapped on my eardrums:

Is it fighting? They're lucky. How did it happen? Poor girl... This type of

101

inaga people! Useless, reckless, daredevil drivers!

My ribs ached. I tasted the salty tang of blood in my mouth. My skin had peeled off in some parts of my elbows and palms; snips of bloodied skin still clung to my body, like weak threads. A crowd had flocked around me. My cyclist was also inspecting himself. The other cyclist, hitherto noisy, sat huddled, his hands on his head. The two bikes lay sprawled apart on the road. A hand pulled me up as I struggled to my feet.

'Are you okay?' a man asked.

I steadied myself by placing a hand on his chest.

'I think...' I stammered.

In the common world of the uninjured, and cannot
Imagine isolation.

Hours later, I met the roadside physician who lived in our street. He gave me analgesic that eased the pain. Blood capsules, even barbiturates. But that night was like a nightmare. I tossed and turned. I cried and cursed. A sudden, awful pain wrenched at my chest. I clutched my Bible and, thinking death had come for me, burst into prayers. Kene sat up on the bed, grumbling quietly. I didn't bother if he was annoyed with me. It was past midnight.

'We need to see a doctor,' he said after I had finished praying.

I was in complete agony. He began stroking my neck, my arm.

'I shall call your office in the morning. I'll let them know you're too ill to get up,' he said.

I crept into his arms. He placed my head on his shoulder, and whispered endearments in my ear. I got a week off. After I had breakfast, Kene scheduled an appointment with a doctor who was once his schoolmate. His boss called him before eight o'clock and requested they meet at the office. It was something urgent, something that needed his attention. He came back late. We couldn't see the doctor. That night the pain was excruciating: I thought I would go insane, but the next morning I woke and felt a strange relief. I imagined I was in a painless world. I ran my hands all over my body, rubbed my chest, squeezed my breasts, and poked my stomach. No pain; I was whole again. I called Kene but he was in the bathroom. When he came out, a towel draped around his waist, looking refreshed, I jumped out of the bed, and threw my arms around his neck.

'It's a miracle. It is gone,' I said with tears in my eyes.

He gazed at me, amazed, then with affection. 'Honeycomb, you are well?' he asked. I nodded. He asked again if I was sure. I nodded again. 'We still have to see the doctor,' he said, and rubbed my shoulders.

'I don't feel like leaving this room,' I said, feeling heat hardening my nipples. 'I need you…' I stuck a hand under his towel and he let out a husky sound.

*

I resumed work three days later. On the fourth day, I began going through an unusual sensation, feeling easily tired, like a pregnant woman, and growing dizzy from walking a few yards to the stop, where I normally boarded the staff bus. I had a premonition that I would pass out soon. And I did. Just on the fifth day, I was waiting for a taxi because the staff bus was grounded. I became unaccountably hot. It was like the sun was right behind me. I looked upwards. But the sun was distant in the sapphire sky. Something was wrong. Was it the weather? Or was it my mind? And I swayed. Then I heard voices, taut. I blinked, squinted at the unfamiliar faces. I was in a stadium as the sounds of man and machine floated all around me, I imagined.

What happened?
Is she ogbanje? Is this a demonic attack?
She has opened her eyes.
Look, she's breathing!
Hey, thank God.
Bah, girls of today. Who knows if she hasn't committed abortion?

Hands, like cockroaches, were running across my body. I realized I was being lifted off the asphalted surface of the busy road. I had collapsed.

The body aches for its mirth
Strapped to the infirm bed

*

103

A rib bone had shifted and pierced through a vessel. It caused a rupture in the pleural cavity. That was what happened the moment I spun off the motorbike and landed on my chest. Intra-pleural hemorrhage, the doctor said. I was placed under observation like a guinea-pig, then infused with some blood and then passed on for surgery. Cardio-thoracic surgery afterwards. Even though I had lost a large amount of blood, I was recuperating fast. I was getting better, yet, my body seemed empty of bones, light as air. I was placed under observation again. This time to 'ascertain your stability,' the doctor told me. I was soon moved out of intensive care unit to a ward occupied by six patients with different health conditions.

Waft me about, O zephyr,
As a butterfly on merry wings

*

Two days before my discharge

Nurse Jane beamed as she entered my ward. It was late noon. The air was moist. It drizzled earlier. From my window, the sun was a smoky ball in the aluminum sky. I could see a bird, a hawk, a kite perhaps, gliding against the white and grey clouds. The bird and the clouds were like patterns in a quilt. Nurse Jane sat down on the edge of my bed. She was young, twenty-something, but she acted like a big sister. And she was quite humorous, unlike the other nurses who acted like every patient was an irritant. Now, she urged me to go for a walk around the hospital premises. I hadn't stepped out of the ward since I was admitted as a patient. I grumbled to myself as I got off the bed. Nurse Jane went into another ward. I picked up my handkerchief and some money. I dressed up.

Outside, the accident scene popped up in my head. That singing *inaga* should have slowed down after the pothole. He would have lain dead had it been a car. I walked down a corridor, grateful that I would be free of the antiseptic odour and the cheerless folks with whom I shared the walled world of the unwell and the dying. Those previous eight days in hospital had been like a sojourn in a cell. Nevertheless, my colleagues had been very supportive. Beverages, cards and other provisions littered my cupboard.

I passed a ward and heard doleful voices. A few persons

surrounded a man lying still in bed. I wondered, just fleetingly, if he had breathed his last. I continued walking. I paused at a pavement and closed my eyes, smiling. Kene would be coming before nightfall. Every day he checked up on me, like a brother. He slept in the chair at my bedside. As a friend he regaled me with jokes, teased me till my ribs ached from laughter. 'Honeycomb' was our pet name.

I sat down on a long bench on the pavement. There was a waiting room a yard or two away. There were elderly people coming out of that room. Thoughts of getting old started to scratch at my feelings. And I wondered if it was selfish if someone took her life before she got to ninety when she was too weak to 'pooh-pooh'.

The panic
of growing older
spreads fluttering wings

Two women came towards me. One was a stout nurse, prim in her starched white uniform, with a stern look on her face that called to mind the image of a proverbial wicked headmistress. The other, a skinny patient, moved slowly behind the nurse. She was clad in a long towel-like dress which made her look like a mannequin in over-sized clothes.

'*Du ngaa,*' said the nurse, pointing to the bench where I was sitting. The patient sat down, not too close to me.

'You can enjoy the fresh air. I'll be back,' the nurse added and walked away. The patient had young brown eyes. But her body was geriatric. As a child, I would have feared that this woman beside me could pass for a witch. Instead of fleeing, I stared at her, thinking I had seen her before. She too was looking at me. Both of us were like a squirrel and a snake watching each other at a distance.

She coughed dryly, her cheekbones rose, and seemed to pierce through the thin skin of her face. There was something allure-like about this patient, something that defied the ravages of sickness, something that gave off an air of fearlessness. She noticed I was still watching her, so she wanted to grin. But what showed on her face was the kind of fixed grin one would see on a Bini bronze head.

Head of a large tuber
of yam. Hair, scant tufts

Fragile

of scorched grass…

I inched away from her. You would never have touched her lips with your finger, even if it earned you a stinging lash on the buttocks. Why didn't the starchy nurse take her elsewhere? I knew what was destroying her life. It was not tuberculosis. I felt brief splinters of ice cut into my flesh. Chilly as the feeling I experienced when a mighty rat rolled over my foot one night.

A bald man hobbled towards us. He sat down on the floor, leaned his body against the pillar, and gazed skywards. He had crow eyes, with a watery hint in them. One would have assumed he was crying. I imagined a haze of gloom hanging above our heads, the three of us sitting in a cocoon of solitude. Someone made a choked sound, a cough, hollow. The type of cough one emits in a room blanketed with thick fumes. It came from the female patient. I began to feel that she might not have any friend or family. Sometimes, I tried to imagine how my parents had died. Were they doused in petrol and set alight? Were their stomachs sliced open like fish? I was familiar with gory tales of massacres in the North, yet, it barely curdled my blood. I believed the demise of my parents probably had made me a little hardy, a little undisturbed by other people's death.

My father and mother used to live in Kano, a land which was known as the 'groundnut pyramid' during the colonial era. Father was a railway worker, while mother was a seamstress (so my uncle had told me). Then, a religious riot broke out at the twilight of the Second Republic incited by some hegemonic Northerners, newspapers claimed. The Arewa were unhappy with the drastic power shift to the South, with the shake-up in the military (which mostly affected the Hausa).

I sighed and gazed at a puddle of water. It was stagnant, greening on the surface, around the edges. It had the ochre tint of urine. I thought of algae and mosquito larvae spawning. A dragonfly appeared, skimmed over the water, rippling its surface, then disappeared.

My land like the Middle East is
a vortex of hate

My parents died in the riot. Houses, cars, shops belonging to Southerners were torched. Men and women were strangled, amputated, halved, or butchered. My father's younger brother came very close to being beheaded by flaming-eyed zealots, wielding blood-stained swords. He was quite lucky. The Sabongari quarters were not readily penetrated: most Southerners who resided there kept handy guns. Before the killings grew wanton, some Christians made it to the barracks. I was among the lucky refugees. Our neighbour's wife picked me up and carried me on her back while the slaughterers raced after the fleeing throng. Uncle Amaechi showed up as my guardian at the police barrack, a month or two later. He had gone round searching for my parents. He found me. Together with his wife and two children, we relocated to the East. I was just a five-year-old then. Uncle Amaechi had visited me twice in hospital, once before the surgery and then four days after. I was consoled that he did not stay away like his pain-in-the-neck wife. She could only send her measly wishes; she never did like me.

I watched a smartly-dressed boy holding the hand of a woman, but he had a worried look on his face. She was bulbous like a sow, and walked stooped, as though a giant abscess sat on her rear. The boy pulled the back door open. Clutching the knotted part of her wrapper, the woman tried to lift herself into the car. A stocky man came out from the driver's seat and assisted her. I was wondering whether the woman was the boy's step-mother, when someone touched my shoulder. It was the skinny female patient. She had shifted nearer, unknown to me.

Buried though in a morass of present pursuits,
The past returns

'You don't recognize me?' her voice sounded groan-like.
I squinted. 'No,' I said, disliking her audacity.
'It is the AIDS,' she said.
I had suspected all along but I was taken aback by the casual tone in which she said it, as though it were Hello. I started wondering whether the disease had eaten away her sensibility.
'You were in IMSU?' she asked again.
'Yes.'
'You don't remember me?'
'Sorry, I can't remember.' Placing her face was like looking for a lost child in a busy market. Her questions were beginning to vex me. I rose from the bench.

But she grabbed my wrist.

'You remember Ijeoma?' she asked.

'Who?' I murmured.

'Ijeoma.'

'Which?'

'Your course-mate,' she answered, slightly excited.

'Miss Peacock. I do remember her,' I said and shook her fingers off my wrist.

The patient was hurt. I made to leave and heard 'your handkerchief'. I looked at her; I didn't notice I had dropped my handkerchief. I took it from her gratefully and suddenly realized that she shared some waning semblance with Ijeoma. I heard Ijeoma had two brothers, no sisters. She probably was enjoying life's sweet *hors d'oeuvre* in South Africa, if she had not relocated to New York or Paris .

'You are related to her?'

'I'm Ijeoma.'

'You...?' I stammered.

She nodded her head.

My mind went into a whirl. I almost reeled from the deadening blow her disclosure dealt to me.

Should I weep for fishes flopping in the Delta of oil?
Or of farms burrowed through by crude pipes of despoliation?

Look at her now! I could make fun of her right away. Recall the bile I had borne against her, how wretched she made me feel back then at university. But something stronger than glee overwhelmed me. Something strange.

How could I accept her in her 'new' looks? Ijeoma was born beautiful. Nothing could wilt her flesh. She was not bony and long like a bamboo, like this sickly female before me. She ought to know I never liked her. She must be very brave to expose her identity, to check her pride, and say this much, without fearing that I would gloat over her misfortune. How could I talk freely with someone whom I had often wished evil? Have you seen an adversary lying prostrate before you? Drawing a deep breath, I sat down again. She glanced up at a group of female student nurses drifting by. They chattered like pigeons, excited. Young just like us.

Where youth grows pale, and spectre-thin, and dies;
Where beauty cannot keep her lustrous eyes

Ijeoma and I should be age mates, 25 years old. Now she looks like a hag, hopelessly aged by AIDS. What happened to those papaya boobs that stoked heat between a man's thighs? Big, firm breasts men once ogled at were now slack and dry, like withered grapefruits. The nurse did not look in my direction as she came up behind her patient. 'You'll need it,' she said and draped a browning shawl over Ijeoma's shoulders. 'So you don't catch a cold.'

'Oh thanks,' Ijeoma said. The nurse stared at me. Her patient told her my name was Nky. We greeted in Igbo. With her hands on her hips, like a female Yellow Fever officer, the nurse asked her patient whether she wanted to go in, as it would soon get cold. Ijeoma shook her head languidly.

'You shouldn't stay out too late, understand?' and the nurse walked off. Ijeoma pulled the shawl tightly around her body and gazed out into the horizon. The sky was aglow with clouds of lily, clouds of lilac. Birds floating like nylon bags, like paper kites in the air.

'When the initial shock left me, that is, after I'd been told about the virus, I began sitting in the patio, dreaming of an after-life where nothing counts, where nothing really matters,' Ijeoma said. 'I would watch the sky turn to gold, and then indigo. I would picture my life blending into their colours. I loved listening to birds singing in the bushes. Also, I would picture my voice mixing with their songs. I own a duplex in SA. That was years ago before the accident, four years ago. I was in Nigeria. I was home for Easter break.'

Four years before, I had been serving with a private media house. That was where I met Kene. Sporty, dressed in white short sleeves and blue jeans, he had come to install some computers in our office, an ultra-modern publishing house. The bald man heaved himself up, then ambled away.

'I'd gone to visit Anne. You may not remember her,' she said. Anne also graduated from IMSU. She did her National Youth Service Corps with a bank. Anne and Ijeoma were very close. She wasn't our course-mate, yet she hung around our classes. Sometimes, she waited outside for her friend to finish lectures. They both gossiped about me. I remembered.

'We still keep in touch. Anne's been an angel. I was driving back to my village after I left her place. Another car bolted out of the blue into mine. That was on Enugu-Port Harcourt Expressway. I was rushed to a nearby hospital...' She paused. 'You are crying?' she asked.

I was not. I just didn't know why tears trickled down my cheeks at that moment. 'N-no,' I said, a tender lump bobbing in my throat. I pulled out the handkerchief and dabbed my eyes.

She touched the bridge of my nose. 'I've always admired you. You were strong, and cool,' she remarked. 'Thank God. I survived the accident. I went back to SA. About a year later, one winter, I was frightfully ill and very cold. Pneumonia, I thought. I was diagnosed. My doctor said it could be managed, though hopeless. It was needless taking an ART. He sounded vague. What do you mean? I asked. I was nearing hysteria. He held my hand and talked about being strong in the teeth of crisis. 'You've AIDS,' he said. I fainted. You know, everyone seems to think I got it through blood transfusion.'

I jerked. The lump dissolved.

'It was critical, and I needed some pints of blood. I was unconscious. I almost died from that accident. It was critical, believe me.'

Hadn't I been infused with blood too? A wild emotion began stamping around, like a restive mare within my chest. I squinted at her, feeling uneasy.

'You don't believe me?' she asked. My mind began frantically searching for the face of the doctor who administered the blood into my system. But fuzzy shapes confronted it instead. 'You think I became loose in South Africa?' I grunted. I wasn't responsible for her actions, so she needed not convince me. It was her life.

Darkness abruptly descended on the hospital. Someone shouted out a name. Someone else yelled, 'Have you changed over?'

Sieve-brained, you think me? -
Don't be puzzled if I see through you
for I wear a mask too

'You were free with guys, you forgot,' I mentioned peevishly, as more shadowy shapes butted into my head. I could not remember the doctor's face, surprisingly.

'None of them saw the colour of my panties,' Ijeoma said. You hardly saw Ijeoma alone. Guys, like bees, kept buzzing around her. So, would you believe she did not sleep with any of them? How could she act righteous even in her poor state? This was no way to obtain sympathy. It was rather as infuriating as when a drug peddler tries to convince you that you can cure malaria from drinking she-goat's piss.

The gurgling sound of a generator lessened my fears and the lights came back on. I assured myself that I could not get positive. The blood was uncontaminated.

'You have to believe me,' her tone was desperate.

'You were famous,' my tone was firm.

'That doesn't mean I slept with men!'

She trembled and then broke out coughing. I wanted to rub her back soothingly, as mothers do when a child is retching. I wasn't sure if I should – or could. I was not even sure how she would react as we were not intimate. I told her, 'I BELIEVE YOU', but I felt she knew I was lying, so I glanced away. The shawl dropped off her body to the floor. I picked it up, aiming to place it back on her shoulders, but she took it from me and wiped her nose on it. I wanted to draw close to her, though I felt a bit uncomfortable. I scratched my head. Was she a virgin? Every student in our school knew she was the irresistible Campus Queen no full-blooded male could ignore.

'That blood was not infected,' she said, sounding as though her nostrils were congested.

'You can't be so certain.'

'I know. I'm certain. I didn't get the virus through transfusion.'

She was trying to confuse me. I knew I had to keep steady.

'How else could you've gotten it?' I asked.

'You may not understand.'

I suddenly remembered that there was something unearthly about her. I had suspected long ago, even when other students were blinded by pulchritude. I observed she was breathing as someone with a boulder on her chest.

'You can trust me.'

She tittered. 'Trust you? Indeed!'

Trust me as a fellow patient at least, I considered saying. That was not convincing enough.

'Tell me. I'll understand,' I said instead.

'I'm not what you think I am,' she said drawing nearer to me. I thought of putting an arm around her shoulder, as a sly gesture that she could confide in me. But I was too anxious to hold myself. I didn't want her to know that I suspected she was from the Sea. *If you see mammy-water, never (you) run away...* I recalled that song, and thought of fleeing. But I did not. I patted her knee. 'I could be of help, you never know.'

Ijeoma stared at me in an eerie way that made my buttocks twitch and my palms sweaty.

'You wouldn't tell a soul if I told you something dear to me?'

'Yes, yes.' I was curious and scared at the same time. If a spirit being showed you her true identity, you either disappeared or died on the spot.

Doubts were troubling Ijeoma because I could see she was finding it difficult to speak her mind.

'It's something I learnt in my secondary school. In the dormitory we girls...' she began.

'Forget it.'

'Tell me,' I insisted, 'Please.'

She seemed to hold her breath a moment.

'I found pleasure in the presence of girls,' she said in a tone that was tense, so inaudible one might miss hearing her correctly.

I arched my brow at her, hoping she would give details. She said nothing more. She bore the face of a mirror, empty of emotion, unfeeling. She did not even bat an eyelid. Her words replayed in my head. What kind of pleasure did you find in the presence of girls? I wanted to ask her. I even tried asking her if she was serious. But my tongue felt like a metal ladle, as I made out what she had implied. And something, like a whisk, began to stir my stomach.

Untie the tongue
Yet, the song is dumb

'I had never gone for a test,' she spoke unhurriedly. 'I didn't have any reason to see a doctor. I couldn't get HIV because I was different. So I believed. Moreover, I'd never fallen sick in spite of the busy scope of my job. I had to shelve my job; my world had collapsed. I grew worse each day. My manager and the agency were sympathetic. A tough decision, but I decided to leave for Nigeria ...'

There is a tale about passenger X who sat beside passenger Y in a car. They began talking. The next stop was X's. Both passengers shook hands. As X alighted from the car, he saw he was holding something, a hand? The lifeless hand of Y. He turned and peered through the window. Y was grinning back at him.

I felt just like X, although I was shaking my head as if I could lose some of the grim revelations Ijeoma had funnelled into my ears. She paused when she saw I was not paying attention. What could have made a girl whom everyone regarded as *le beau ideal* turn into a deviant? I had always known something was wrong with her, but never did I expect her to be... different!

'You have some money?' she asked.

I looked at her. She pointed to a boy carrying a large pail of Pure Water on his head.

In the streets
the African child,
the leader of tomorrow,
how he hawks about

I called after the boy. He came towards us, barefooted.

'Is it chilled?' I asked.

'Aunty, it's chill well, well,' the boy said bringing down his pail.

I stretched a hand and felt the sachets lying among chunks of ice. Cold water dribbled through my fingers as I offered a sachet to Ijeoma. I took out a rumpled N5 note and paid the boy. As he walked off, I wondered what his parents were doing at home. She bit off a tip of the sachet. Some water splashed onto her face.

'Shit!' she spat.

'Ndo, sorry,' I sympathized.

She sucked the remaining water from the sachet. Her face showed a deep frown.

'It has a taste.'

'The State Water Board is still on strike,' I said. 'One can't be sure of the source of water one is drinking nowadays.'

'It tastes bad, sour.'

I said to myself, life is sour.

'Don't sound cynical.'

'What?'

'I heard you,' she said.

'Oh,' I said, just realizing that I had voiced my thought.

Ijeoma threw the sachet away.

'It wasn't Anne,' she began speaking fast as if to spit everything out of her chest. 'Cleo is one kinky fairy of a girl. She is fun, but sleeps with men. We quarrelled several times. Lorraine is sort of a live-in mate, cool-headed. And there is Omphile. She has feisty Italian blood. Lerato – she is as erotic as her name. Lovable Olivia. It could have been any of them.' Ijeoma closed her eyes.

I thought she was brooding over her past. Without opening her eyes, she went on, 'It's said the virus from an infected partner can seep through tiny bruises in one's mouth. When one brushes one's teeth, the gums often get injured a little. I don't know; so they say. I remember hearing something like that, something about the mucous membrane in one's lips. I mean, when you engage in cunnilingus.'

My head throbbed as I tried to make sense of all she had been saying. This was quite a shocker. So she was this way at university? So some of those girls were like her? I could not even think of any reason for her not being straight. I tried to imagine her in bed with one of those girls. I could only see the blurry shapes of a man straddling a woman in an X-rated movie Kene and I watched one weekend, as a storm stripped the night of its serenity. I couldn't imagine another girl fondling my bare body, her tongue writhing between my legs, licking me up.

As she opened her eyes, her lips began to tilt wryly, like she could discern my thoughts, like she was about to laugh at me. 'Shades,' the word came out slowly, as though she was trying to make out the title of a book or recite a poem perhaps. 'Shades of days kissed by the sun. Hmm… someone said, life is a mirror. Rather an inapt metaphor. I can only say life's one goddamned delicate piece. Mine was a mirror quite all right. I didn't take a look in it. I see my reflection in people's eyes. You think it's now fragments?' she fixed her eyes on me.

I should sound reasonable. Yet, I found myself wandering in a maze, getting more befuddled. Her revelations were hard knocks on my head. 'This AIDS business is a mystery,' I said.

'It is more like a curse on mankind,' she said. 'Remember that lousy course in Greek Mythology? The gods play with earthlings. Zeus couldn't hold his randy dick.'

I laughed quietly. Ijeoma continued after a long pause: 'It is not easy to hold fast to something that's breakable. Trying not to give up, when all round you everything speaks of death. You hear groans that chew your heart. One sees adults crying on their beds. You think of taking your life every so often. Why did I return home? Why did I not stay back...?' Ijeoma sounded subdued. Sadness shook her voice. Her eyes seemed rheumy. She lowered her head as one who was drained. I realized I too was feeling subdued. Would she break into tears? Was it not better if she stopped talking?

Ghosts of the past
hovering birds of prey...

Yet, she chattered on, 'I've hushed up loads of things. Anne alone knows all of them. I wasn't supposed to say anything. I'm surprised that I told you our most precious secret. Anne would feel vexed. We've been dear friends since secondary school. It seems strange, my lifestyle, right? Well, all this started one rainy night. We found out that girls cuddled one another whenever the rain pounded on the roofs of our dormitory. Anne and I shared the same bunk bed. When we started shivering like drenched birds, we would just cling to each other; that way we warded off the cold. It started harmlessly. We were two innocents and never thought it was abnormal. At university, we realized some girls were like us. They made us feel it was a sisterhood kind of fun, feminist stuff. Nothing to be ashamed of, but we had to be very secretive. Anne and I believed we could always drop it when we had had enough of it. Men desired us, pined in their fantasies of us, but then, we deprived them of the pleasure of taking off our underwear. We gave them kisses on the lips, on the cheeks, but then that was nothing. It was fun to see men burning with lust. We felt extraordinary, powerful. I'm talking Greek, right? I just have to get all these fucked-up secrets off me. I always wondered what knowing you would have been like. You don't mind me saying that, do you?'

I did not have enough strength to even get offended. I was still befuddled.

'My loving parents could no longer carry the shame. If I'd married an *osu* they would have tolerated me. But telling them my secret (she touched her groin), they would run mad. I placed myself in their shoes. No one could bear the thought of their only daughter dying of AIDS. It was better I kept my lips sealed. I can't go back to SA now. So, I say to myself, better dead among the dead than at home with the living.'

'Don't they know you're...?' I asked.

'That's sprinkling salt on a sore. It is safer they assume I was promiscuous.'

I rubbed my arms and wished I had worn a sweater. I thought of the blood that was transfused into my body, once again, and prayed it was uncontaminated.

'Anne's been very supportive. She'll be here tomorrow with her fiancé. You'll like to see her?'

I said nothing. I did not consider meeting any of her 'friends' as interesting as they may be. I didn't want to encourage her to start having any whim. I should be leaving tomorrow if Kene agreed. I was downright bored with lying in bed and fed up with inhaling odour as stomach-churning as fermented cassava.

Let it go, let it flow,
Like a mighty rolling billow

'They deserve to know, right?'

'Who?'

'My parents, I've disappointed them,' her tone was lachrymose. 'What's the point? I'm dying. I shall tell them. I can only hope they'll still accept me as their daughter.'

The despair in her voice yanked at my heart. Although she was trying to appear cool in the face of death, she looked pitiable. Did she know beforehand how she would die?

I wasn't bothered anymore about the how and the why of her life, how she got infected, why she turned lesbian. I did not want to appraise the fatal relationship between the virus and kissing. Or oral sex, either. I could not believe a girl so beautiful and full of promises could die that easily, like a rose blossoming with strikingly crimson petals, but only to be crushed by an angry gardener. I felt the need to cry. Cry loud and long. Those grudges I had carried in my breast all that time. It appeared Ijeoma was about to cry instead. She raised a hand, but it fluttered over her face. Then, suddenly, she gave a strained sound, a gasp. She gasped again, her features tensed, her back arched. She was dying?

I wanted to scream for help, when she sputtered, 'I'm okay. I'm okay.'

I began to pat her gently on the back, asking her if she wanted water, if I could fetch the nurse, if I could take her back to her ward. She said nothing. I wished I could read her thoughts as an amiable silence rose between us. Like a glassy pane shielding one from foul smoke, it was unnecessary breaking it, with speech. We would never go through this rare silence again, I knew.

The song is of silence, harmonious and a balm to the heart strained too tight

The atmosphere was surreal. The sky was a dusky sea. Stars looked like sardines. Crickets had begun chirping. The hospital was getting bare. Most invalids had gone in. A sprinkling of visitors and staff still shambled around. Motorcycles horned outside the gates. Voices floated intermittently in the air. There was an aloof expression on her face. I could see Ijeoma had decided to live with her fate. No regrets. Nobody would make her feel guilty, worthless, or gross. She did not need pity anymore: she wanted ACCEPTANCE.

'I've a confession to make,' she said.

My heart skipped a beat. 'Not shocking, I hope?' I asked.

'I did find you attractive.'

I frowned.

'Not what you think,' Ijeoma added. 'You were brilliant. I deliberately sat next to you at lectures. I wasn't brilliant like you. I was smart enough to know that good looks could get one anything. I exploited it. You were cold, always so cold. You looked down on us. You were only being proud.'

'*O bu asi!* That's not true!' I said. 'I wasn't the person who won the coveted crown.'

'But you were focused. Annie and I talked about you.'

'I agree. I was only attempting to steal attention by making bright...' I stopped as I heard Kene's voice.

'Honeycomb, what are you doing out there by yourself?'

Kene hurried towards me. He made me feel like a little kid who had to be protected from strangers whenever he was around.

'Hello honeycomb,' I said in a coo, readying for a hug.

He wrapped me in his arms. 'You got me so worried.'

'I know.'

Kene released me and squatted in front of me, holding my hands.

'I just spoke with the doctor…'

I placed two fingers on his lips and said, 'Meet Ijeoma, my former course-mate.'

Kene glanced up at her; he actually hadn't noticed her. Now he almost flinched. He straightened up. As he moved towards her, he stuck his hands into his pockets.

'How're you?'

'Horrible,' she said.

Kene and I shared embarrassed glances.

'You fell for it!' Ijeoma said with a slight laugh. 'Don't mind me, I'm fine.'

Kene and I smiled. He told me to carry on with our girl talk and promised to wait for me in my ward.

The lyre of love unfurls myriad notes
Of fluttering joy and peace!

I watched Kene disappear down a lit corridor. I could feel some warmth caressing my navel even as a chill swarmed all around us, even as mosquitoes buzzed about our legs, like street beggars.

'Is he your boyfriend?'

'Yes.'

'You love him?'

'I used to resent you,' I answered instead. Her expression darkened and I wondered whether I had offended her. I went on, 'I became so frustrated I prayed something nasty would happen to you. I couldn't see any reason why you should enjoy all the attention. I felt you didn't deserve it.'

She reached for my hand. Without thinking, I curled my fingers around hers.

'Can you forgive me?'

'Nky, I'm glad we had the opportunity to talk,' she said. Then she drew two invisible rings in front of her eyes with her other hand.

'What?'

'I mean, where are your glasses?'

'Don't remind me –' I sounded vehement. 'I chucked them into the bin!'

'But they were cool on you.'

'Those bottles made me look like an owl.'

'You now see clearly?'

'I squint.'
'I noticed.'
'Is it obvious?'
'Yeah.'

Even as night wove its spell of gloom
The larkspur of dawn blossomed still

We were giggling like two naughty teenagers when the headmistress-looking nurse returned again. She told her patient it was almost 8 p.m. The generator would soon be switched off because the diesel was rationed. I remembered the labour was on strike and the government was busying gadding about. We both had to turn in.

'How do I look?' Ijeoma asked me, somewhat impishly.

I saw in her eyes the high-spirited course-mate I once envied, but whose sincerity and courage I now admired. I now realized that I, too, had craved acceptance in our university days, although I'd refused to admit it.

'You look…' I held my mouth.

'Frightening? Depressed?'

'No, you look contented,' I said.

'That's what I think,' Ijeoma said.

I dropped my hand. The nurse helped her to stand up.

'Nky, it's been a pleasant evening, right?'

'Yes, yes, Ijeoma.'

She held out her hand to me.

I wanted to hug her. Clasp my arms around her. But I acted self-consciously, timidly, in the presence of the nurse who was pricking me with the suspicious eyes of a warden.

'I'm happy we met.'

'I'm happy too,' I said, finally shaking hands with her.

'Take care then.'

'Bye.'

The nurse held her by the wrist. My skin turned pimply as they began to move away. I would not see Ijeoma again.

'*Cherie!*' I sprang off the bench.

They both turned back.

'Can I see you tomorrow?' I asked, hugging myself, trying to fight back the tears that filmed my eyes.

Fragile

Ijeoma hesitated as if the idea unsettled her.
'I'd love to see you again,' she replied and smiled.
For the first time I saw her teeth. They were no longer sparkling
pearls; they were now the whiteness of watery milk.

Born of the mellow womb of moon
her smile melts through the shelled heart

No Woman Left Behind
Tolu Ogunlesi

'No.'

That was all that Modinat said when Soji approached her and tugged at her wrapper. The lights were out (the latest blackout was already two days old), and the candle in her room had burnt itself out, so all she could make out was the outline of his body, a black, familiar statue.

Then she realised that 'No' alone was the wrong thing to tell her husband.

'Please, we must use a condom,' she quickly added. In the darkness, even though she couldn't see anything, she knew that she wasn't merely imagining the look of surprise on Soji's face. The shape in front of her seemed to step back, to shrink a little into the darkness. When it spoke, it did so in a voice that did not seem to come from it.

'Condom?'

'Yes...'

'But we didn't talk about condoms yesterday, did we?'

'I know, but...'

'When a wife is asking her husband for condoms, what should a prostitute be asking for?'

Solape, their four-month old baby began to cry.

'Your baby is crying. Go and take care of her.' Soji turned and merged with the darkness.

*

Modinat could not sleep. She lay there, long after Solape had fallen asleep on her milk-engorged breasts. She laid the baby on the bed beside her, against the cold wall, and reached out to feel her nose, buttoned-up mouth and fingers balled up into a fist with an energy that belied the age. The wonders of infancy, that brief time of bliss before real life arrived to violate innocence. She sighed again, and turned onto her side, as though to throw a new invitation to sleep to come and redeem her from the turmoil that wakefulness was stubbornly spoon-feeding her with.

She kept wondering if she had acted rightly. It had never happened before – this turning down of Soji's demand. Not even when they were still befriending each other, when she was learning fashion designing at Abule Ijesa and he was an auto-mechanic who had just gained his freedom and was looking for funds to set up his own workshop.

And Soji had always wanted sex often, so often that Modinat had had to ask Nike, her best friend, how often she and Walata, her boyfriend *did it*. Nike had first eyed her suspiciously; sex was not something they ever talked about.

'How often we do it?'

'Yes. I have my reasons for asking.'

Nike had shrugged and said that, well, it was difficult to answer. 'You know how men can be, if it sparks in their head they will be asking five, six, even ten times a day; other times their mind is blissfully filled with other things like Premiership or money.'

That wasn't particularly an answer – but it was helpful. Modinat had smiled and thought to herself that perhaps Soji was a bit unusual then; even with the English Premiership on his mind, even when Arsenal lost a crucial game, there always seemed to be a chamber in his head reserved exclusively for sex. At six months into her pregnancy he still attempted to climb her, until her mother provided a solution.

A tiny quantity of a local red dye that she was to discreetly spill on her thighs the next time Soji approached.

When he screamed, she screamed louder.

In panic he almost lifted her up in his arms. She insisted that she had to clean up first, before they went to the hospital, and she had her way. At the General Hospital, the nurse gave them two options – either they waited for the Doctor, he was out for lunch and there was a full waiting room already; or they allowed her to see Modinat and if she saw that it was truly an emergency, she would get the doctor to attend to them urgently. The first option would cost them only the price of a hospital file; the second would quite naturally cost a bit more.

They settled for the second option.

'There is no problem with your wife,' the nurse declared, after an extensive probe in an empty side-room that Soji suspected was kept empty for situations like this. It had a bed with a stained mattress on it, and a cupboard stocked with bandages and syringes and other medical supplies which all carried conspicuous price tags.

The nurse saw that her flippant-sounding verdict was not going to allay Soji's worries. So she disappeared for a minute and returned clutching a yellowed paper that looked like it had only recently been laminated.

'You are educated *abi*? So you can read. *Oya*, take.'

It was her Nursing Council Certificate, certifying that she was a qualified Midwife. 'Sometimes you people just think we nurses don't know anything. You think if you don't see doctor you will die. If you don't see doctor you haven't come to the hospital. Look, with this my hands I have delivered more than two hundred babies – whether mother or baby, God did not allow one single one like this to die in my hand.'

*

Modinat thought of going to Soji's room, wearing nothing but a wrapper, and allowing it to slip off her back as she climbed into the bed beside him. That brief thought aroused her in an almost violent manner. She thought of apologising to Soji, telling him she was sorry, she didn't know why she said what she said, she wasn't feeling well and didn't know how to tell him, she...

But she changed her mind. She had made a decision, and she had to keep to it. And then she remembered that Solape's *Babeena* had almost finished. And there was a doctor's appointment next week that had to be paid for. She didn't have any money, like many other women in the area all her eggs were in the basket of NOWAL – No Woman Left Behind, the American micro-finance NGO that had started tutoring them on owning and running small scale business and had promised that funding would soon follow. NOWAL had been quiet in the previous few weeks though. The training sessions had dwindled and the white men and women appeared only rarely, like ghosts.

*

Earlier that day, Modinat had taken Solape to see the doctor to complain about the rashes that kept appearing on her face and chest. As she sat in the crowded waiting room, taking in the myriad smells of stale wounds and unwashed bodies and drying bodily fluids, someone poked her. Wearily, she turned to see who it was. It was Mama Titi, their former neighbour. Talkative Mama Titi, who always knew which husband was about to leave his wife and which child had started smoking *igbo* unknown to his parents, and what the latest style of tying *gele* was, even if one *gele* was all she could afford for a long time. Mama Titi who had lived with her five children and husband in a single room downstairs, until they moved out into their own house – six bedrooms it was said to have – weeks after the husband won a councillorship seat in the last elections.

'Ah, Mama Titi. Long time.' Sitting on a wooden bench for two hours, holding a restless baby was turning out to be more tiring than walking about.

'You! You just forget me *sha*!' Mama Titi said, poking her in the ribs again. 'Come on, get up and come and greet me properly *ojare*...'

That was one thing with Mama Titi, she was ever cheerful. Even when she got annoyed and would rant and cuss and lash out, it didn't require any serious effort from her to resume her cheerful mode soon afterwards, which was why her nickname – even though Modinat refrained from calling her that, as she was much older, by at least five years – was 'Mama Nothing Spoil.'

Modinat dragged herself up from her seat, even though she had been worried that someone else would take it if she stood up. Mama Titi was not the kind of woman you turned down. No. Even if you hated what she was making you go through, you smiled while hating.

Mama Titi saw the fatigue written all over her. '*Pele*, eh...that is children's *wahala* for you... one moment they are smiling and playing, the next moment they are turning the hospital to your second house...'

Mama Titi was fond of her because Modinat had always been kind to her when they had lived in the same house, never failing to loan her Maggi or candles or kerosene, or even the occasional scoop of Vaseline or toothpaste.

Mama Titi took Solape from her and within seconds had strapped her onto her own back. 'Come with me Modi, let me see, there is a nurse that I know here, her husband is Baba Titi's boy, she should be able to help you see the doctor quick quick.'

With that, she marched off with a burst of manic energy. Modinat followed, each step making her feel like she had exchanged legs with an elephant.

Mama Titi slowed down suddenly and drew Modinat closer. A hospital trolley swung past at that moment, dragging a hospital maid along, narrowly missing Mama Titi's foot. '*Oloshi*, you should have let that thing hit me eh?' She dragged Modinat to the side of the corridor. 'There is one thing I have to show you Modi, before we go and see this nurse. Come with me…'

Off she marched again, squashed against her back a now-smiling Solape.

'Let's stay here. We can see well from here. *Oya*, turn this way, no, come and stand here. Look, *ehen*, over there.'

Modinat still didn't know what this was all about. She hated wandering about in hospitals because that was when you stumbled upon corpses being wheeled past and accident victims dripping flesh and blood.

Mama Titi was pointing discreetly at a large hall metres away from them. 'Can you see that room, eh? Okay, what you will do is this… you will walk past the door as if you're looking for somebody. Just look inside quickly and go on your way, then turn back and come back here.'

'Mama Titi, na mortuary?'

Mama Titi chuckled. 'Mortuary *bawo*? If na mortuary you tink say I go dey here… even when my father died I didn't follow them to the mortuary to go and see his body, *eemi*? Just go and look first, it's not the mortuary…'

Modi shrugged and moved unenthusiastically in the direction of the hall. From the outside it looked like a restaurant. There were people going in and out – young girls in tight-fitting jeans, men in suits who looked like they had just stepped out of the office, women in brightly-coloured boubous, clutching babies.

'You know that place you just saw, Modi – that is the H – I – V Clinic!' Mama Titi announced when Modinat returned. She spoke with the excitement of a radio deejay unveiling the Number 1 song for the week. The way she fixed her gaze on Modinat's face she looked like she was eager to see how much of an impact her statement had made.

Modinat looked confused.

'Modi! H – I – V. AIDS.' Mama Titi lingered on the 's'. 'Do you need me to explain that one to you again? Even me, old woman like me, I know what HIV is!'

'Mama Titi, I'm not saying I don't know what it is' Modinat said, almost indignantly. 'It's just that….'

'It's just that what? I am telling you that is the AIDS clinic. All those people you saw there, all of them…'

Modi gasped. Not a loud, dramatic one, but a gasp all the same. She turned back to look in the direction from which she had just come.

Two hours later, as she left the hospital premises, Modinat ran into Banke, Soji's ex-girlfriend, whom he had been unable to marry not because they fell out of love but because they had both been carriers of the sickle cell gene. After years of holding out and hoping for a miracle, they eventually broke up because they were not prepared to risk bringing a sick child into the world.

Modinat was going to walk past and pretend she didn't see Banke, but she saw that it would have been hard to pull it off. So in that moment of awkwardness made further awkward by the fact that there was nothing to justify enmity between them, they acknowledged each other. Banke stopped just long enough to tickle Solape's cheeks.

Modinat's own policy was that there's something about keeping your friends close but your enemies even closer.

It was as she stood at the bus stop, in the throng of sweaty Lagosians waiting listlessly for *danfos*, that the thought first hit her: what had Banke come to do at the Hospital? Then she thought of the HIV/AIDS Clinic and shivered. She shook her head violently and told herself she was just being stupid, but the thought would not go away. And why did Banke not ask her about Soji? There'd only be one reason for that – she was seeing him regularly. Modi imagined herself mentioning to Mama Titi that she saw Soji's 'ex' at the hospital gate. She knew what Mama Titi would say and exactly how she'd say it.

*

Once in a while Modinat would take pains to sniff through Soji's pockets, sometimes when he took his bath, or when he was away at the neighbourhood bar in the evening, after he returned from work and changed from his clothes into the jeans and T-shirt he usually wore later in the day. And every now and then, when she borrowed his phone to send an SMS when she didn't have credit on her own phone, she made it a point of duty to check his call and messaging details.

Not once had she seen any SMS from a woman on his phone, and he never kept his sent messages. All the messages in his inbox were from his clients, messages chock-full of car models and spare-part names and pick-up times for broken-down vehicles and this-is-what-I-can-afford quotations. And they always happened to be from men.

Didn't Soji have any female clients? He was an honest, hard-working, knowledgeable mechanic and he got a lot of referrals, so... Or did he delete all messages from women? Why? Even female clients?

Once, she copied down an unsaved number after noticing that a couple of calls had come in from it over a two-week period. The following morning, she went to the phone booth down the street in order to call the number. She knew she had only one chance, so she had to be smart. When the call went through, she assumed a nasal twang, wordlessly cussed her thumping heart, and said 'Banke, good morning.'

The person at the other end said that she wasn't Banke and she didn't know anyone called Banke.

*

Mama Titi's last words – just before she left Modinat standing on the hospital corridor, watching people come in and out of the HIV Clinic – kept ringing in her ears. 'In this day and age you're allowing him to rush you with a naked organ? See this girl, are you sure you want to live long? See all those small small girls and boys coming out of that place, who look even more well-fed than you, will you believe if you see them outside that they have HIV?'

Modinat didn't know what to say. 'Mama Titi, what can I do? We have never used a condom before! How will I say it? Our marriage is only one-year-plus...'

'Look at me, eh? Baba Titi dare not bring his *thing* near me without wearing rubber. Me I don't care. If he wants, let him carry it outside, me I will protect myself...'

'Mama Titi, it's not that easy, you know… you've been married more than ten years… your husband can't be disturbing you as if you just married yesterday.'

'Look at you, this girl. You don't know anything about men. Whether seventeen or seventy, they're all the same.'

The morning after the condom incident, Soji got his bath water himself. He ate his *akara* and *pap* in silence. Unusually, his transistor radio stayed off, casting a weird silence on the parlour, a silence that seemed oblivious to the sounds of crying babies and metal buckets and revving engines outside.

Modinat felt uncomfortable, and more than once she felt like dropping on her knees to ask Soji to forgive her. He dropped some money on the table and stepped out. Moments later she heard the roar of his Volkswagen Beetle and the familiar rattling sound it made as it ambled slowly in and out of the mini-gullies on the road past their house. She strapped Solape onto her back and walked to the phone booth, feeling like she was carrying the burden of the entire world, not merely a baby. She narrated what happened to Mama Titi.

'If we start fighting now, how will I do it? He's the one taking care of me and Solape…'

An unruffled Mama Titi gave her an appointment at the Council Secretariat for ten o'clock that morning.

*

At seven minutes past ten, Mama Titi and Modinat marched into Baba Titi's shabby, but pompously decorated, office. When they walked out fifteen minutes later, Modinat had a job. She would be joining the motley crowd of female toll-collectors lined up against the broken-down front fence of the Secretariat. There was a dirty, cramped crèche within the secretariat where she could put Solape and check up on her as often as she wanted.

Modinat was not sure that Soji would allow her to work in such a rough job. Everyone knew that council workers – at least the men – were touts and petty criminals, while the women were merely big-breasted, bleach-burned versions of the men. But there was plenty of money to be made, in commissions and diversions, and the last thing Baba Titi told her was that she was 'on her own', and that she had to make sure she didn't act 'slow-slow'.

Mama Titi expounded on what her husband had said, but not before stepping out of his office. 'Look, Modi, as a woman, you cannot depend on your husband for everything. If so, you won't have any voice at all. You will just be there, waiting for him to bring his penis to your bed every night. Let me tell you, and you're the only one I'm telling this, I collect contracts from the Local Government, I supply air-freshener, supply typing paper. Baba Titi doesn't know, he doesn't need to know. When I finish building my house I will let him know. It is not as if I want to move there, God forbid. I will only rent it out and become Madam Landlady.'

Modinat wanted to ask Mama Titi if she had this same confidence back when things were tight for their family, when all seven of them lived in one room and her husband rode an *okada* to make ends meet. She wanted to ask if Mama Titi had insisted that he use condoms back then. Most importantly she wanted to ask Mama Titi if she was pregnant. The way her tummy was looking…

*

Two evenings later – evenings in which Soji did not approach her for sex (which was strange, as she couldn't remember the last time they went three days without sex) – as Soji sat down to eat his supper and listen to the nine o'clock news, Modinat bustled about in the kitchen agonising over how she'd tell him about her new job.

All day she had battled with doubts about the job. What if NOWAL resumed their work and then told her she was no longer eligible for a grant because she now had a job? And why did she think that getting a job and making money for herself would make her husband respect her opinions more? And, to be honest, what was there to be afraid of in AIDS? Everyday young people were dying from accidents and armed robbers; spending all of their brief lives worrying about contracting AIDS did nothing to ward off the ever-present shadow of death by other means.

Then she thought about something she had heard from a female congregant at Firepower Ministries Inc, a Pentecostal church that Mama Titi had once taken her to. This woman had come up to the pulpit to give a testimony of what God had done in her life. She told of being long past the age of marriage (the handiwork of her mother's step-sister who cast a wicked spell on her) and suddenly – after being prayed for by the General Overseer of Firepower –

finding herself faced with marriage offers from two men and in desperate need of divine guidance.

'I told God, "I will call both of them on the phone now. The one you do not want me to marry, let his phone be switched off,"' the woman narrated to an enthralled audience. It worked, she explained, as one of the two phones was off. She married the other man. And now she had been married to him for six months without them arguing even once.

When Modinat heard it, she thought it sounded rather like gambling under the cover of God's Name. She whispered this to Mama Titi right there and then, where they sat together in the overflow section of the Church, watching proceedings on a large television screen. Mama Titi dismissively whispered back something about God working in mysterious ways His wonders to perform.

Now, months later, Modinat thought an idea she had once discredited might be a good way to gain divine clarity in the midst of her confusion. With her hands trembling, she dialled Mama Titi's number. It rang at first, but no one picked up. When she tried it again, it was switched off.

Apparently, God had not run out of mysterious ways to guide men. And women.

Modinat packed all the unwashed plates into the sink, soaked them in water, switched off the kitchen light, walked into the sitting room, and stood there, watching Soji watch television, thinking of how she'd ask for his forgiveness.

She had never found herself in this kind of situation, in which she struggled to find a way to start a conversation with her husband. It was just like being a seven-year-old once again, running onto the rotting wooden quay in Gbeku, the village where she grew up, watching the overloaded school boat dance dangerously on the water as it sailed away, oblivious to the fact that the little girl left behind would be writing a promotion exam that morning.

'Soji, please, we need to talk,' she said.

MY LITTLE STREAM
Soji Cole

It was my most carefully considered opinion. Democracy has not really yielded the desired results in the country. The evidence laid before us as the car bumped into yet another pot-hole. I felt giddy and dreadful. The driver turned his head slightly.

'Sorry oga,' he offered

'Oh! No sweat,' I replied, trying hard to impress him with my *been to* attitude. We had been on the road for about two hours, from Muritala Muhammed International Airport in Lagos, heading to Ikirun in Osun State. We were going towards Oshogbo and I had taken my time not to miss a single thing of what democracy had helped to develop in my country. I found it hard even to blink. I thought I would catch a little sleep in the car after the tiresome flight, but my quest to see what the country looked like after twenty years since my departure kept me awake. Even if I tried to sleep, the jerky exercise that came from negotiating one pot-hole on the road and bumping into another would certainly make a vigil necessary.

Certainly, I saw changes; virtually everyone was brandishing a cell phone. New buildings with sophisticated architectural designs had sprung up. The evergreen forests on the highway from Ibafo in Ogun state to Ibadan had yielded to Pentecostal villages. More cars and more hold-ups on the roads. There was greater flourish and grandeur in the cities, but not in the eyes of the people.

Muji's many mails to me had contradicted my imagination. Her letters had left me with the impression that Seattle, where I stayed in the United States, was, after all, similar to Nigeria. My problem started when I discovered that one of the cubicles at the airport, where I was finally able to clear my luggage after hours of delay, was enraptured in darkness. I couldn't help asking my new friend.

'Why was that bit of the airport in darkness?'

He turned his head slightly, a usual habit of his that I was beginning to despise. I hadn't come all the way from Seattle for a careless driver to kill me in a crash, but his firm authority on the steering wheel soon reassured me.

'Oga, na so dis country be now o,' he said. My questioning face probed further. 'Before, before, na light for morning, no light for night. Later, the tin change to one day off one day on. Now na no day on, all day off,' he enthused as he negotiated another pot-hole, almost hitting a careless bike rider who chose his way. He readjusted his head, hoping to continue.

'Alright, I understand,' I quickly stopped him. I saw his expression in the mirror. I really didn't care. I had grown to fancy my life and I would do everything to keep it safe. I am not always interested in drivers who are chatterboxes, especially behind the steering wheel. But, sincerely, I understood him. A friend of mine had hoped to return to Nigeria five years previously in order to continue his business. He had complained about the heavy taxes in Seattle and had made plans to relocate to Nigeria. He gave a lavish party on the eve of his departure. Two months later, he was back in Seattle! He had settled his tax problems and continued his business. From his account, I learned of the failures of our leaders and the darkness which the country had been plunged into. Yet, Muji kept writing to me to come back home and establish myself in the country. Thank God I was only visiting. Really, I had missed my siblings, but that was not enough reason for me to come back and plunge myself into a system I no longer understood. That was not even enough for this visit. I talked with them all every other day on the phone. I had arranged for my mother to visit me in the United States twice over the previous three years and I was regularly sending money home to aid my siblings. I was visiting just for a purpose, a purpose known only to me: my little stream!

I remembered with fervent nostalgia my little stream. I recalled my many forays with Ronke - that childhood girlfriend of mine, with tribal marks lavishly sprawled on her face. Her halitosis is something I definitely wouldn't like to remember. I sincerely pray she's a mother now. No time for crude reconciliations. My little stream is anxiously waiting for me. The stream had given me the fondest memory of my life. It was just a few meters from my house. My mother would walk towards it to shout out my name when other children had already retired to their homesteads, enjoying their supper and listening to moonlight tales of the tortoise and the hyena. She knew I would be there. She had carefully studied my infantile itineraries. Whenever I received some sound beating from my mother or one of my uncles, (my father seldom beat me), I would run to My Stream and she would be there to wash away my tears.

My friendship with the stream began the day I saw shoals of tiny fishes happily swimming while I was having my bath. All the children had their baths in the stream. The adults used the improvised closet beside the mud kitchen. I stood there watching the fishes, water dripping from my naked body while the racing altocumulus added to the enchantment . I tried to take some of the fish in my cupped hands but they slipped through them. I was at this game, quite oblivious of the passage of time and of the impending rain. I was utterly transmuted. My nearest such encounter to nature was when I planted two grains of corn in my pot. I saw the seed germinating three days afterwards and my happiness was such that I gave my supper that evening to my gluttonous brother. I hid the pot carefully inside the kitchen, covered it with a rusted trestle, and watered it every five minutes. I wouldn't be done until the germinating seeds were covered with water. I wouldn't allow my first creation to be starved. Four days later, they were dead. I hadn't known known the tricks of photosynthesis. I cried in the kitchen, like I was bereaved. It was two days later that I courted the stream. And there I was, trying to catch the fishes and quite unaware of my mother's calls. Her heavy slap on my naked back jolted me from my reverie. That night, even father had to join in beating me.

Afterwards, I would use every excuse to be at the stream. I always wanted to wash the dirt off my body, but when my mother discovered the trick, she sanctioned my bath and pegged it at twice a day, at the most. I would take over Muji's chores of looking for the stray fowls at dusk and bringing them home. Once again, mother, not one easily to fall for a fast one, barred me from touching the chicken coop. I would kick the improvised ball I was playing with in front of our house out of view, hoping that the other boys' attempt to retrieve it would take me out of my mother's vigilant eyes. But there she was, her eyes permanently fixed on me. In the end, I broke into a spate of unmitigated defiance. I would run out of the house at random, especially when she was busy in the kitchen, and went straight to my stream.

And there it would be, waiting for me to come for the usual consort. I would watch the stream lapping gently at the rock in the middle. The encounters with the fishes had become friendlier. I would catch some in my cupped hands, having learnt the logic of their slippery tricks. I would throw them back into the water when the water with which I collected them had sapped out of my hands and the hapless creatures were beginning to flip about and gasp for breath. I would watch with keen alacrity as the young delicate crabs that had ventured out of the undergrowth struggled to resist the mild tide. Once, I saw a snake meandering its way up through the climbers and out of view. I hated snakes with unremitting passion but its presence would not make me desert my stream. I would collect the shimmering coloured sand at the bottom of the stream with my hands, separating the minuscule shells and saving them in the tiny tin box which I had picked from the tinker's shop. I remembered the day I collected three fishes in the box. I couldn't sleep all through the night. I was on top of the world. I hoped to keep them until they were big enough to eat, then I would present one to my mother as a gift. We would have a good dinner with it. The other two, I hoped to keep until they procreated and the cycle would begin again. I stuffed the tin box with enough food for my fishes: yam (both raw and cooked), cocoyam, rice and other food items I could scrape particles from. The next day, the three fishes were as lifeless as a stale pudding. I was sorry for taking the poor creatures out of their natural habitat only to have them killed. Tunde, my friend from the house next door, suggested I threw salt into the water in order to bring them back to life. I ran to the kitchen, scooped a sizeable portion of the salt that had mixed with a bit of palm oil, and threw it into the tin box. One of the fishes wriggled for a few seconds, then lay still, completely inert, probably far more dead than the other two already were. I never attempted to take them for keep again.

*

I was jolted out of my reverie. The driver had bumped into yet another pot-hole. Actually, he couldn't have avoided it, as we were now in the untarred section of the road that leads out of Oshogbo to Ikirun. My good friend was quick to notice my fright.

'Sorry Oga', once again he offered his unsolicited recompense. I may have caught the figure of a clown when I jerked off my mental recapitulations. This much was evidenced by his synthetic expression as I noticed the smile on his dimpled cheeks. Well, I didn't care. I had mine on him too. In twenty minutes, I would be home. Home to my people. Home to my stream. He would have to return to Lagos immediately and I would never set my eyes on him again. I could arrange my return back to Lagos.

*

The fresh smell from the forest on either side of the road revived my nostalgic meditation. I recalled the day I first met Ronke in the stream. I really didn't know why she had come up again in my thoughts. I really don't need to fear anything. I am a free citizen of the world and I can think or imagine anything. No law places embargo on thought, and by the way, no lady in such rustic set-up would wait for a man for twenty years. She would probably be nursing her seventh child by now. Family planning is an obscene lyric in the ears of my people. But what if she's still single? I remembered that day, in my infantile amateurism, I had promised to marry her!

I thought of that again, of the day I met her for the first time. All enraptured in my semi-conscious state within the stream, I had heard something suddenly being dropped in the water. It had brought me back to life. I assumed a twig may have got broken and splashed in. I went back to my rapturous reverie. The suddenness with which the second splash occurred threw me into a spasmodic fear, especially as no one was about. I had heard tales about esoteric creatures who made their abode in the innermost recesses of nature, deep inside the thick forests and the quantum silence of the sea's abyss. Yes, I was told that, occasionally, they do wander out of their conclaves in order to behold the spectacle of human activities. I looked about once again: no one in sight. It registered fast: they were mostly invisible to human eyes except to one who underwent a ritual transfiguration. Only then one would be able to see, communicate and even compete with them! But there I was, completely helpless and lost, confounded by the thought that the spirit might even be the wicked one that eats up children fast! My kinetic was totally suspended. The fishes were nibbling lavishly at my static feet. Then the laughter came through. I turned and there she was, coming out of the bamboo thicket she had been hiding in. She was indeed a creature, not as much as those eerie beings I had feared, but as well as a human contrast. Some parents are absolutely satanic! The tribe marks ran through all available spaces on her cheeks, sparing the eyes and nose as boundaries, then extending to the forehead. The marks formed such deep trenches, enough to hold rain water, that I wondered about the butcher who got the credit. I tried to hide my initial fright.

'You weren't told not to intrude where big men were having...?' she cut me short with her laughter. I fumbled. I stood there like a fool, like a mannequin I was to see fifteen years later in Aberdeen. She saw through my fear. I wanted to charge and smack her, but her undulating voice stopped me.

'I just wanted to come and play with you', she ignited my fury further. 'My sisters are washing over there and they would not allow me to touch any of the laundry, so I decided to play away'. I looked into the direction she pointed and indeed saw the sisters by the other edge of the stream. They must have been looking at me for a while, for, by then, they were grossly engaged in their laundering. That infuriated me even more, really, but not as much as this girl's irritating accent, putting 'sh' where the letter should have been 's' and subverting 's' with 'sh'. Who the hell is this adventurer that explored the tropical forest to come out with this...?

Her mien dampened my fury. This girl with the outward appearance of an orphaned orangutan actually had the nature of an angel. We did not stop talking until her sisters beckoned to her that it was time to leave. I felt lonely after she was gone. I had never felt that adult-like in my life. She found her way to the stream the following day and that was when I promised her marriage. We kept a regular communion afterwards until I became the best student in the local primary school, got the lone scholarship to the government college Ibadan, which was ceded to the village, and eventually won the federal intermediate scholarship that took me away from the country. I didn't want to imagine that I would get to the village and would see her, only for her to remind me of my promise. She should have understood in the later years that those were childish wish-sayings. Children are violently susceptible to fantasy. Though I am yet to marry, my life plans do not include bundling a modern homo-habilis back to Seattle. I live a sophisticated lifestyle over there and I wouldn't... But what was I thinking? For twenty years I didn't suppose she had made progress in life as well? I may as well be surprised to learn that she equally left and studied at some top rate university abroad or at one of the five universities in the country. By then... Yes, by then I would start considering... only if her accent and halitosis were gone and she'd be ready to meet one of the world's greatest plastic surgeons in order to rid her of her facial...

*

'Please stop!' A sight had caught my eye and banished my recalled memory. Some people were crowded trying to buy something from an elderly woman. A glowing fire raged from the mud hearth in the middle of the scene. The smell slowly sifted to my nostrils. I remembered this sight very well! This same spot and almost about the same time of the day! Nothing had really changed, except that the woman had grown old, twenty years older, and the set of people crowded around her were unfamiliar faces. That was Iya-Ibeji, the woman who sold eko and akara, a local combo-delicacy of cold corn gruel and fried cake made of ground bean paste mixed with spices. I had known her for as long as I could remember. I told the driver to reverse. They came in full view. We had entered Ikirun, my hometown and place of birth!

The tears slowly welled up into my eyes. I was gripped by an undefined nostalgic tension. I wanted the things that had formed my childhood experience back. I wanted to race back twenty years of my life! Definitely, I would have my own eko and akara later, not now. Someone would have to come for it. I told the driver to move on after giving him the route to our destination and the instruction to go steady, at twenty kilometres per hour. I wanted to savour all I had missed during those years. I wanted to see the joke that democracy had played on my village. I wanted to see how much my people had caught up with the global race. I had a deep sentimental attachment to this place that even my twenty years outside the country and eight years of permanent residence in Seattle had not managed to erase.

The brownish mud houses had stood rigid all these years. Only few of them seemed to have had their roofs changed in recent times. There were occasional concrete houses that had sprung up here and there, upsetting the balance of the brownish shades. I saw some children and women crowded round a concrete slab. I told the driver to stop again. I probed my sight further. They were fetching water from a borehole tap. The girl whose turn it was to get water was battling with the manual pump, a protruded iron pipe jerked steadily up and down before the water could come out. I read the large notice mounted above the facility: GOVERNMENT ASSISTED WATER SCHEME. I came up with the realization that we had not really got it right with democracy. It is the government's responsibility to provide such facilities, but the impression given by the mounted notice was that a special favour was granted to the people. In fact, the world had gone past these types of projects which required you to be fully fed before using the facility. The manual exploration of the facility was an archaic idea. We had public taps in Seattle but they were something much more worthwhile, and you rarely ever saw a crowd about them, because the system had made things so convenient for the people. This was absolutely a mockery of my people's poverty and helplessness. Twenty years earlier, we got our drinking water from the stream and we hardly ever heard of water-related ailments.

The driver proceeded at my behest. I saw the local primary school I had attended. The mud buildings were still there, defying the passage of time. As I looked on, making no attempt to clear away the hot tears sliding down my cheeks, I saw the message they were trying to pass onto me: *never be shaken until it is absolutely over, stand your ground even if the conditions are not favourable.* Though they had rigidly stood their grounds, one couldn't help but notice that they were whittled down, one of them almost split in two from the constant bashing at the hands of the weather. I saw the goats moving gaily up and down, enjoying their own turn to use the classrooms. They had always been the classroom occupants after school hours each day and even considered them their exclusive reserves at weekends. I remembered every Monday, after the roll calls, how we would go into the classrooms to sweep off their frosted dung and wash off their strong smelling urine that had congealed itself on the floor.

I saw some boys kicking away a plastic ball in the small field and a group of others acting as spectators or waiting their turn to be part of either team. A goal would determine that and the potential team member would remove anyone he felt like from the team that had lost. We moved on towards home. In another seven minutes I would be in my house. In less time I would see my stream. My eyes caught another sight: a motor park! I remembered that where it stood now used to be the wasteland which housed the shrine of the egungun masquerade. Now, here is a motor park, with people and buses. Had the egungun spirits relocated? I thought we were told several times that they came from heaven and were much more powerful than mere mortals. They probably relocated to a more serene environment, trying to catch up with globalization. I was aroused by guttural voices surrounding the car.

'Baba alaye!'

'Area father!'

They were about six of them. I asked the driver what the hell was happening.

'Oga, dem be area boys o,' I learnt that they were garage touts who jumped from working in the garage to every other means of earning a living.

'So what do they want?' I asked with no attempt to hide my disgust. I had to part with a thousand naira before they left the car. I just couldn't bear their guttersnipe lack of decorum. Their expression of gratitude was even more irritating than the initial harassment. They were almost rolling on the road, jumping about, clearing the road for my passage and one was even cleaning the windscreen of the car.

'Is this what they do every time?' I asked.

The driver, obviously displaying his anger at my overwhelming generosity, told me the money I had given them was too much. I should have given out just a hundred naira. I wondered how a hundred naira would have been sufficient for five hungry men who compromised their dignities and pounced on you to part with some money. To my driver, it was not a matter of dignity at all. None of them would have earned a hundred naira in a day. In fact, he made me realise, by insinuation, that I had given them just half of what he would be paid for his efforts for bringing me from Lagos to my village. He could as well have made a better living just by playing sycophant like the area boys if everyone that passed by were as generous as I had been. I made up my mind to pay him three times the amount charged on my conveyance. I knew the money charged would go to the airport taxi company where he worked but I would give him double that as personal incentive or 'tip' anyway, as it wasn't wrong to use the word in this country.

My heart raced as I saw something in front of me. That was where my stream was supposed to be! I asked the driver to move a bit further and park. Yes, this was where my stream was! I couldn't believe the spectacle in front of me. A small bridge had been constructed over the stream. I got down and moved towards the stream. No, it couldn't be. My inside revolted like a startling fusillade. This couldn't be my stream. It must have shifted ground, just like the egungun shrine. Then, I saw the rock still standing defiantly in the middle of the stream and the mystery came to an end.

The bridge had taken away the natural scenery which attracted me to the stream. The climbers had gone off. The bamboo thickets around it had vanished. I moved further and climbed down beside the bridge into the stream. There it was! Probably the most unfriendly sight I would behold in recent time. A side of the stream had turned into a waste heap, emitting an offensive odour. Some pigs were dipping their snouts into the dirt, quite oblivious to my presence. I looked into the water but my fishes were gone. The crabs must have been evicted as well. The stream itself looked narrower than it was when I left it. I was furious. My little lovely stream was gone, and in its stead laid a catalogue of disgusting debris. I stood there, staring vacantly, quite unconscious, as what remained of my little stream swallowed and carried away the tears from my eyes.

Haunted House
Alpha Emeka

Jonathan had just started walking when my father celebrated his sixtieth birthday. It was three weeks before Christmas and the smell of the season was strong in the air. The occasion was meant to be a big one but Jonathan's mother, Kate, thought it would be better low-key. Kate was the twenty-seven year old woman that my father impregnated outside wedlock and then brought home and made his fourth wife. She was five years younger than me.

My father had never taken anybody's opinion seriously. Kate came into the family and changed all that. Now he doesn't make any major decision without her consent. Kate was the kind of woman who spoke her mind and damned the consequences. My father liked this, but for the rest of the family, it was hell. Everything about Kate was humiliating.

I knew Kate long before I travelled to the United States. She was fresh out of secondary school then and had just gotten admission to study Sociology at the University of Calabar. I was a student of Political Science at the same university. I was living in the student's quarters in Etonko, where Kate used to live with her boyfriend, James. James was a junky. Once he had enough of the drugs and her, he'd start to beat her. We got used to hearing Kate scream in the middle of the night. We had advised Kate many times to leave James but she had refused. By the end of the first semester of her first year, she had had a black eye, a scar on her jaw and a few bruises on the left cheek. That was my last semester at the University and the last time I laid my eyes on Kate, until the day I saw her in my father's house.

When I graduated, I did my one year compulsory youth service and left for the United States to further my education. I was in the United States when I heard that my father had taken another wife. It all sounded like a joke to me. The day my father called me and asked me to congratulate him, something within me told me he had gone crazy. I congratulated him as he requested, but he knew I did not approve of his decision.

The relationship between my father and I had been nothing short of cordial, but my father never disclosed to me the circumstances surrounding his marriage to Kate.

'Mayor,' he said on the phone one day, 'I want you to come home, I will celebrate my sixtieth birthday in grand style and... I want you to be there. I want all my children and grandchildren to be there... I will invite the President, the Governors, the Local Government Chairmen, the Council of Chiefs, Traditional Rulers...' He kept going on and on and on. My father was a Governor in the Second Republic.

When I got tired, I asked him to stop. 'Okay, okay, okay, dad, I will be there,' I said. That was all he wanted to hear. He hung up.

I made my preparations and within a fortnight I was in Nigeria. My father was on hand to receive me at the airport. My siblings George, Joseph and Grace were also there. It used to be better when my mother was alive. She would dance and wave her hands in the air and thanked God for the journey's mercies. My favourite part was when she asked God to give us the wisdom to invent alternative means of travelling to the US. It's been five years now since she died in a car accident on her way to her friend's wedding in Badagri, yet, it all seems like yesterday.

My father's house appeared deserted when we drove in our convoy of two hummers. Only Musa, the security man who opened the gate, could be seen.

'As I told you on the phone, Mayor,' my father spoke suddenly, 'this house belongs only to me now; me and my new wife. I bought a house for your mother downtown. It is equally as big and as grand as this. You can stay there if you want, if you don't, you can check into a hotel, I'll pay. After all, I was the one that invited you. I also bought a house each for my second and third wives. I want peace to reign.'

There was silence as the car stopped and we all got out. The bougainvilleas, roses and hibiscuses in the compound had been trimmed perfectly, but the leaves of the short trees fluttered to the waves of breeze passing above the fence, reminding one that they still awaited the masterly touch of the gardener. My father sometimes called him The Master Gardener but his real name was

Obong.

'You're welcome, sir, you're welcome,' the security man said with a broad smile that exposed a set of teeth that were red with *gworo* or kola nut.

'Musa, you have not stopped eating gworo,' I said.

'I will neber stope,' Musa said with a Hausa accent, still smiling.

'Where is Obong?'

'His wife born pickin' and he go and see them.' Musa waved his hand in the direction of Obong's house.

I turned towards my father sharply. 'I stopped counting when Obong had eight children.'

'Ah! Obong have ten children now…' Musa said and spread his ten fingers towards me. 'This one make it eleven.'

'Jesus!' I exclaimed. 'Why is Obong –'

Musa did not allow me to finish.

'Ah!' he exclaimed again, 'I have –' he spread his ten fingers in the air and bent down and joined them to his toes and then rose and nodded his head in satisfaction.

'You have twenty children, Musa!?' I exclaimed.

'And pour wives now,' he replied.

'This is ludicrous!'

My father quickly changed the topic. 'Come,' he said, 'we have so much to talk about.'

Birds sang in the trees as we talked and laughed and headed towards the main entrance to the house. Just as we were about to enter, a woman with a baby in her arms appeared from the hedges on the left side of the compound. It was Kate, the girlfriend of the junky, James, I left way back at the University of Calabar. I stopped dead. My father, George, Joseph and Grace also stopped. They all stared at me while I stared at the woman approaching from that side of the compound. 'What's she doing here?' I asked in a low tone. My voice sounded more American than I ever let it.

'Ah! You must pardon me. I did not know she was in the garden,' my father said. 'Please meet –'

By then, Kate had recognized me and had taken a few unsteady steps backwards. She almost dropped the baby in her arms.

A feeling of suspicion that she was my father's new wife crept over me. 'What's this bitch doing here?!' My voice had reached the high heavens.

'Don't call my wife a bitch!' My father roared, a most unexpected roar.

I turned slowly to look at him. A horrible silence descended. The trees rattled with a wave of breeze, the birds stopped singing and flew away.

'This bitch, your wife...?' I asked in a low tone. My eyes had become watery. For the first time, I noticed my father's defenses fall. 'This bitch your wife?' I emphasized, nodding my head in anguish. I turned automatically and headed towards one of the hummers. 'All of you, let's go.' George, Joseph and Grace quickly followed me. I almost hit Musa as he quickly opened the gate and I drove out of the compound with a screech.

Everyone was silent as the car purred through the busy roads.

'My brother,' Grace said suddenly and broke the quiet, 'How did you know that gold digger that calls herself Kate?'

Grace was sitting at the front, beside me. George and Joseph were sitting in the back. 'Yes, brother, how did you?' They both said at the same time and promptly leaned forward to hear the answer to their question. My mind dwelt completely on their faces, my father and Kate. I was looking for a connection between the two of them. 'It doesn't make sense,' I concluded aloud, 'It doesn't...This is absolute ludicrous. Dad has gone gaga.'

'Slow down a little bit,' George said. 'Don't forget that you're in Nigeria now. The roads are narrow and busy like the market place.'

I quickly stepped on the brakes and the car slowed down.

'You haven't answered my question,' said Grace with a pleading voice.

'Oh, yes, sorry. I knew that bitch way back at the university, in my final year to be precise. She just got admission and was sleeping with one junky named James every night. After fucking her, the crack-head would beat her and she would scream until dawn. That scar on her face is as a result of one of those nights of fucking and fighting. She's a wild bitch.'

'Oh Jesus! This is worse than we thought,' Grace said and slumped back into silence.

'Dad is a fool!' George exclaimed suddenly.

'Wake up guys, he can afford it!' Joseph said. 'He still boasts that we will not be able to finish in our lifetime all the money he amassed when he was Governor in the Second Republic!'

'The money he looted, you mean!' George corrected.

'I was just trying to be polite you know!' Joseph said.

'Guys, do you remember that day he told that South African embassy official that he could move the whole of his family to the seven star hotel in Dubai and live there for ten years if he wanted?' Grace said. 'Dad still got money stashed in bank accounts we don't know about. That whore will dig really deep if we don't do something about it soon.'

George snapped his fingers in the air. 'You want me to fight for looted money? God forbid!'

'Looted money or not, it's our money now and we have to protect it! It's not our fault that looters go free in this country. It's not our fault that integrity died and was buried at the end of the civil war! Dad is a great man as far as I'm concerned,' Grace said. 'The problem now is that he does not do anything without consulting that whore!'

'How do you mean?' I asked.

'Whose idea do you think it was to buy a house for mum and the other wives?' replied Grace. 'The first day she arrived at the house, she had an argument with dad over us. Before long, she stormed out. The next thing we heard, dad was looking for a house to buy for us in the other part of town.'

'What!' I exclaimed and banged my fists on the steering wheel.

'Have you heard?' continued Grace, 'Dad's sixtieth anniversary will now be low-key, thanks to Kate.'

At this point, I could not keep focus ahead. I swerved the heavy hummer off the road and screeched to a halt. 'What did you say?' I asked Grace.

'Yes, she has pressured dad into keeping the occasion as quiet as possible. No more media coverage, no more high-profile guests, just the family and a few very close friends and relatives. There is nothing we didn't tell dad to make him stick with his initial plans but he refused. It's unbelievable.'

'She wants to protect her past at the expense of dad's reputation...? I'll not let that happen.'

'That girl is really clever,' said Joseph, 'I now see why she was fighting tooth and nail. Too late, her past has just come to haunt her.'

'What was she expecting when she decided to marry an ex-governor?' George said. 'Brother, you have to tell dad everything you know about that girl.'

I thought about it for a while and then turned the car around with force. All the cars on the road stopped with a screech. Some people in the vicinity turned admiring eyes in the direction of the hummer. Those who turned angry eyes hissed and raved as I pressed the windscreen button and waved an apology. 'Useless people! They'll steal our money, use it to buy big cars and then come back and hit us with it. What will a poor man do in this country?'

The voice of a man trailed the car as the windscreen went up.

My father's hands were around Kate when we drove into the compound. They were holding each other tightly in an embrace and talking to each other desperately, the way young lovers do when they go through the first trial in their relationship. It was the most embarrassing sight. When they saw us, they quickly disentangled and my father began towards the house like a mad dog.

'Guys, this is not the right time,' Grace said passively. Almost immediately, Kate began to wave us away.

We knew our father too well to stay and wait for him to come back. We have seen him shoot a business associate on the leg before for losing three million Euros in a business trip to Germany. I quickly reversed the car out of the compound.

We could only catch a glimpse of the barrel of his Kalashnikov before we disappeared from the vicinity.

The birthday was low-key, like Grace had said. Only family friends, a few friends of my father and neighbours were in attendance. No business associates, no government officials, not even the press was there to cover the occasion. It was a disgrace for a man of my father's status to celebrate his sixtieth anniversary in a quiet and uncolourful manner like this in this part of the world. Yet, the look on Kate's face was that of satisfaction. A mocking smile appeared at the corners of her mouth as she looked in my direction. It reminded me of the old Kate who was beaten and battered by the junky. This new Kate is a lot older and wiser. And with a man like my father by her side, no one dared lay hands on her. I turned and left the sitting room. I went into the garden, away from sight, and sat in one of the chairs. The breeze was gentle; its sensation on my skin was soothing. I closed my eyes and fell into a short sleep. When I woke up, the sight of Kate's baby, Jonathan, playing with one of the two goats a friend had brought as a birthday present to my father caught my attention. He had called the goats 'Arabian Goats' as he handed them over to my father. At first it seemed like a very dangerous play and I wanted to call Musa to carry the baby away from the goat, but the animated play soon held my attention. Jonathan had climbed the back of the goat and was trying to ride on it like it was a horse. The goat promptly shook him off its back and he fell into the flower bed and began to laugh. Still laughing, he quickly reached out and held the tail of the goat and the goat dragged him out of the flower bed.

I held back the feats of laughter. It could ruin the little fun. Jonathan became more excited and wanted to climb the back of the goat again but the goat would not let him. His entire attempt to climb the goat was to no avail; he knelt down and began to beg the goat. At this point I could not hold back any longer and I burst into uncontrollable laughter. The laughter was so loud and so sudden that the goat and the boy were startled. I saw Kate getting out of the house and going mute, as she could not see me. She lifted the boy into her arms and went back inside.

When I got back into the house, I was more cheerful. I caught Kate's gaze twice. It was obvious from her expression that she was trying to figure out the reasons for my sudden cheerfulness. That did not bother me.

I had an urge to look for James and ask him to tell me all he knew about Kate and why he beat her all the time. That urge was soon eclipsed as I got a call and had to travel back to the United States the following day.

I stayed another seven years in the US before coming back to Nigeria. A lot had changed. Kate, my father, and everyone else in the family: they all looked older. My father's house had a new look too, as did my mother's. They were now covered in glossy, cream paint rather than in the former, drab browns-and-whites. The country too seemed to sport a new look, as I found more people with cheerful faces.

The day I saw Jonathan, I nearly collapsed. Although, he was seven years older now, strong and agile, something about his face startled me. He was a carbon copy of his mother's ex-boyfriend, James. 'That bitch has checkmated herself!' were the words that came tumbling out of my mouth. The urge to find James and bring him home to reveal Kate's unfaithfulness now became stronger than ever before. I quickly alerted Grace, George and Joseph and they supported the move.

I made a few calls to old friends; no one seemed to have seen him in the last ten years. I drove straight to the University of Calabar, to his last known address. There was a hair barbing saloon there which he visited all the time in those days. The barbing saloon was still there but the name had changed. The new boy I found told me that the former owner had died three years previously.

At this point, there was nowhere else to look. It was a hopeless quest.

I drove back home, but the thoughts would not leave my mind. After a few days of pondering, I decided it would be better to ask Kate directly about him. I chose the day that my father was out of town to meet her.

My father's house was quiet as usual. Kate was in the sitting room when I came in. She was reading an old magazine. When she lowered the magazine and saw me, she froze for some seconds before stuttering a greeting. I did not reply.

'Where is James now?' I asked. I avoided a direct stare as I threw my hands behind me and began to walk around the room like I was the king of Brunei.

Kate did not utter a word, she kept staring at me. After a while, she regained her composure. 'What do you want?' she asked.

'How dare you ask me what I want?' I said. My voice had risen. 'I asked you a question!'

'I don't have the answer to your question, so please leave.'

I glared wildly at her. I wanted to grab her with my bare hands and break her into two, but I chose calm instead. 'That boy looks like James,' I said.

'And so...?' she replied.

I was silent for a while, 'That is to say that you and I know that you've been playing a very big prank here,' I said.

'You're absolutely correct,' she replied. 'What can you do about it?'

'You wait until my dad comes back, I'll give him the full story.' I made towards the door.

'There's no need for the trouble,' she replied. 'He already knows!'

I stopped dead, too stunned to move further. I turned slowly. 'Yes,' she continued, 'he knows everything. It is you who needs to be informed. Now, let me inform you. That boy is your father's grandson. James is your father's real son; James and the baby growing within me.' She paused as if in a sober reflection. 'Jonathan is the son of James and James is the son of your father, he is your brother. Have you seen the connection now?' She began to cry. 'He killed her and buried her in Government House!'

'Who killed who?' I asked and drew closer.

She looked away and the crying intensified.

'Who killed who?' I demanded.

'Your father killed his mother,' she was gnashing her teeth now.

'Whose mother?'

'James's idiot!' she yelled. 'He was the Governor then and your mother was the first lady. He was having an extramarital affair with the young lady. After James, she became pregnant by him again. When he began to treat her bad, she stormed the Government House one quiet afternoon and threatened to make the affair public if he abandoned her, her son and her unborn child. When she saw that that did not move him, she threatened to expose his drug business.' She looked up at me. 'Your father is a drug baron,' she said in a quiet manner. 'That alone, touched him, so,' she continued, 'he pulled out a gun and shot her on the spot, in front of the little James. That is horrible, horrible!'

She screamed and went silent.

'One day, James became very ill and needed an urgent operation. We didn't have any money so he asked me to go and collect money from his father. When I got to this house, the only person I saw was your mother.'

'You knew my mother?' I asked, shocked.

'Yes,' she replied. 'I told her why I had come; she was sympathetic to our plight. She was a very kind woman. She gave me all the money I needed and offered to drive me to the hospital. She said she had heard about James before but had not met him. When we got to the hospital, she asked James about his mother and James gave her the gory tale. She was shocked. She said she saw fresh excavations in Government House around that time, and that her husband could not offer any reasonable explanations for them. She had let the matter die for the sake of peace. She promised us that she'd go back there and dig and if she found any bone in that site, she'd get your father arrested for murder. That was the last time I saw or heard from her. James was shot three times on the head a week later as he was about to be discharged from the hospital. I was pregnant with Jonathan. I began to look for your father everywhere, to have my revenge. Finally, we met. A friend of mine was the one that did the introduction. He liked me instantly and took me in. I planned to kill him the next day, but it would have been too obvious, so I decided to take my time to avoid arousing suspicions. It was the mistake I made. I discovered a week after we met that he was already dying, he had cancer of the lungs. Cigarettes were already doing the job for me,' she paused, 'but I'll still kill him before the cancer does…'

She was still talking when the door creaked open and my father walked in. An AK 47 assault rifle was firmly in his hands. 'You dare to come to my wife in my absence?' He asked. His voice was loud and clear.

I was staring at him, petrified and unable to utter a single word. Kate went numb with fear. My father aimed the gun at my leg and pulled the trigger. The gun exploded one. I felt my left knee shatter. I screamed and fell to the floor. Kate was shaking, I was shaking. We heard Musa's voice asking frantically; 'Any problem?!' My father swung the gun around instantly and two powerful explosions rocked the house. Musa screamed and an ominous silence descended. My father turned again. A wild grin was on his face now. 'How dare you come to my wife in my absence!' he roared.

'Dad, it is true you killed mum!' I cried.

'Did she tell you how your mother wanted to kill me? Did she?' His voice made the whole house tremble.

'Dad, I'm so disappointed in you.'

He roared with laughter. 'You are just a little boy. What do you know about life?'

The rug was soaked with my blood now. I tried to stop the flow but the pain was too much. I looked up at my father; his gun was still pointed at me, 'Are you going to kill me too?' I cried.

'I have many sons, Mayor, I have many sons. I can always tell the world that armed robbers attacked us and I managed to escape.'

'You're a lunatic!' I cried.

'You're correct. Can't you see that only lunatics make it in this country? Can't you see it's a mad country?' He raised his gun again. 'Goodbye Mayor, you've been a wonderful son.'

I heard the sounds of two explosions again and I felt the bullet pierce my rib cage twice. I slumped back. I felt a strange sensation. Even as I closed my eyes, I could still see. I saw myself lying still on the floor, in a pool of my own blood, I saw my father rain bullets on Kate, I saw the police arrive and I saw my father tell them how armed bandits had stormed his house and had killed his family members. I saw Grace shoot my father twice on the head in front of the police. I saw the police take Grace into custody. I saw my mother, I saw James, I saw Musa and I saw Kate again, alive and well. We all live together in this house now. Number 4 Zang Close is now a haunted house.

GUITAR BOY

Emmanuel Iduma

Perhaps he wished that the man he had killed was only sleeping, and that he would wake up only when he had married her and their marriage was beyond dismantle. Or perhaps he felt justified that he had killed *for* her, and would marry her without the fear that anyone would wake up.

Perhaps he would return to her only once and say goodbye. If he did return, he would pick up his guitar first and strum it quietly, for the last time. Because he planned to leave it. Because he wanted to start a life without it, a life the guitar could not control.

Perhaps the darkness did not meet him leaving the night, without his guitar or baggage. Or perhaps he was not leaving, only letting the city become a blur in his memory, a deep hole that he could fetch from whenever he chose. If these things had happened, then there would have been a story before he killed the man. Only if all of this had happened.

Twenty-Four Signs

Before Higo started working in the place called Twenty-Four Signs, he had lived with his mother few houses away from the military cantonment. His father had died there. He had been a captain. The day he died, the walls reverberated once, then twice. A loud noise was heard. Then the walls caved in on him. He died in the toilet of the Officers' Mess. The news was everywhere; there had been a bomb blast. And the Captain was amongst many that had not cried.

The men came again and again to his mother, because, from what Higo gathered, she had been a Beauty Queen in the secondary school where she had met his father, and the beauty was not gone with age. There were just two rooms in the house he lived in with her. One of the rooms was their bedroom, the other their parlour. The men that came again and again went into their bedroom, sometimes leaving their green berets in the parlour. At those times, he would sit in the frontage with the guitar his father had loved and played. The nights would resound with the proficiency of his fingers. The men always met him still playing the guitar and some complimented his proficiency with crumpled currency.

The day he left his mother was the day she told him she was getting married again, and then she asked him what he wanted to do with his life. He had left secondary school the year his father had died. It was three years later and he had not found his way into a university. Higo looked at her and saw nothing of the mother that existed before his father died.

'Why are you looking at me like that?' She asked him.

'What has happened to you, mama?'

She looked away from him and then sat down. The question she had always seen on his face had finally been uttered.

Simply, she said, 'Oh God.'

'What?'

There was no response from her. Instead, she fondled one of the green berets forgotten by the men. Higo never forgot that moment with his mother. The green beret and the muteness. When he thought about what she said next, the words seemed like a blur but the green beret would be very bright and vivid. She said, 'I did not love your father. I married him because everyone thought I would be a fool not to marry someone with so much money. Now that he is dead, you think I am different.'

Silence hung and though they looked at each other, the green beret lay between them. She picked it up again, fondling it, and saying, 'Lai has always been there. Even before I met your father. Lai was married, but he got a divorce and we are going to get married.'

He said nothing, but watched her fondle the green beret again before leaving it and walking away, inside, where minutes later he could hear her sobbing.

He ruled the night with his guitar, especially the night his mother said she was getting married again. The sound from the guitar was awkward, not mournful, and perhaps soulful, or perhaps its genre could not be identified. When his fingers became sore, he stopped and watched the distant stars, wishing that his guitar could carry him there.

But when he finally got tired of staring at the stars, he picked his guitar and the beret his father had worn, a green one too, and walked inside.

That was the night he decided to leave.

*

Twenty-Four Signs was owned by Mr. Fanon, a European that got finally tired of doing business in Lagos and was moving back to his country. He had poured his whole life into the restaurant, made good money, and was satisfied. Yet, he could not bear losing ownership. He knew more money could still come. Then he found Mr. Rahl, an Indian who had started a restaurant on the next street. He begged the Indian to manage Twenty-Four Signs. Mr. Fanon could not trust a Nigerian. An Indian, who had left his country to do business, was a better option. The European handed ownership to the Indian and returned to his country.

The Indian loved music, good Nigerian music. Before long, he had acquired a piano, a drum set and an acoustic guitar. The vacancy was placed for three musicians who would be fed, paid and housed.

*

Higo found that Mofe was more beautiful than the rest of the waiters at Twenty-Four Signs. Soon, they started sharing words. Before long the other musicians began taunting him about her, calling her his wife.

Their closeness tightened and she began spending hours in his room, especially when she was on the night shift. Higo usually played into the night, for it was mostly at nights that people needed music while they ate.

One evening, she told him why she always wanted to be close to him. 'I like you very much. Very much.' Higo smiled and started a silence she did not break.

But Higo did not think about Mofe's words. In his room that night, after the music had ended, with his guitar resting beside his bed, he thought about someone else. He had met her the night

154

before.

'My name is Candida.'

'What kind of name is that?'

'My father is a South African.'

'What does the name mean?'

'I don't know. I didn't care to know. Why should I care to know?'

'What are you doing in Lagos?'

She smiled. And he still remembered the smile. The dimples, the face creasing in its softness, the absence of lines on her face. She had said nothing about her stay in Lagos, nothing about her ancestry. He thought about her head filled with buildings of South Africa, and if she had been born during the racial violence, he wondered what images would run through her head. And then he thought about how impossible it was to know the images that ran in another person's head.

'What is your name?'

'Higo.'

'What kind of name is that?'

'You know 'Things Fall Apart?''

'What is that?'

'A novel. By Chinua Achebe.'

'No. Is your name a novel?'

He had laughed a nervous laughter.

'In one of the editions of the book, Aigboje Higo wrote the introduction. I loved the book when I was young. So my mother thought the name was good for a nickname. I love the name now. But my original name is Ikechukwu.'

'What do you mean 'original name?' Is there a name that is fake?'

'Yes. Like Higo. Like Candida.'

She smiled again. This time he remembered he had wanted to put his index finger into the dimple and let it swim there forever.

'So you like the name Higo?'

'Yes.'

'Why?'

'I like it because it makes me think I would be part of success, like Higo was part of the success of Things Fall Apart.'

'Very funny. Both the name and reason for it.'

That was the last she said. Bollie, the musician who played the drums, joined them. He had brought Candida. Soon, they disappeared together into Bollie's room. Because his room was opposite, he thought he had heard their ecstasy in the night when he lay to sleep and there was silence and he could only think of her.

He met Candida again the morning after Mofe had said she liked him, at the entrance to the restaurant.

'Oh, I have forgotten your funny name.'

'Higo.'

'You live here?'

'Yes. The room opposite Bollie's room.'

'I see. Is he in?'

'I don't know.'

There was an air of pomposity in her gait and it annoyed him. She said nothing but walked towards Bollie's room. He wanted to call her and tell her he had not forgotten her funny name.

It was Mofe that told him she was afraid of her house. She had come the night after Candida had walked away from him.

'What do you want me to do?'

'Nothing. I want to sleep here.'

'Why are you afraid of your house?'

'I see things there. Sometimes it is a white pussycat. Other times I feel someone pressing me in my sleep. I cannot stay there. The house is evil.'

He closed his eyes and thought.

'You have stayed there for long and suddenly, it is evil. Let me take you back to your house.'

'No.'

'You cannot sleep here.'

She walked out of his room.

But she came back again the next day, with a bag, heavy from its contents.

'What is the meaning of this?'

'I told you my house is evil. It collapsed yesterday night, while I was in the restaurant.'

'What do you mean collapsed?'

'Are you new in Lagos?'

'I want to see it.'

'Do what you want. But I should tell you something. You think anybody wants to live in a house that when it rains bowls are kept everywhere to stop the rain from destroying things? You think anybody wants to live in a house with constant smell of urine because the latrine is bad and the backyard is used for urinating?

And you think I like a mud house that can easily collapse, a mud house that was built because someone was so desperate and could not wait to get money for a better one?'

When she said all that, he suddenly felt tired. He knew it was true that the house had collapsed. He knew the usual story of the collapse of a house; rumbles everywhere. But it was not the collapse of the house that he thought about. It was not even the addition of her to his room. It was how the collapse of a house in his city could influence his personal life, how Mofe suddenly became his roommate because of the collapsed house.

'Please,' she said later after unpacking.

'What? Did I say no? You can stay here.'

'I like you very much.'

He smiled at her insistence, at her voice. Because the sun was already red-coloured, he picked his guitar and walked out of the room. But soon he came back, perhaps because the insistence in her voice kept nagging him, in his head. And he asked, 'Why do you like me very much?'

She told him her story. Her story about the boy that loved her, but she did not love. Her story of their six month relationship and the evening she told him she did not love him. Her story of how he had cried that evening, and how many days after he kept coming and begging. Her story of her continuous 'no' to his appeal. Her story of being raped, one evening, while she walked alone on an errand for her mother.

In her story, the boy that loved her had shown his face when he overpowered her with the aid of his masked friend and raped her. In her story, she became pregnant and refused to abort. At the end of her story, she gave birth to the child and then her mother accepted responsibility while she looked for a way to make her life useful.

After the end of her story, she said to him, 'So, I like you very much because I want to make my own choices. And you are the person I have chosen to like. All my life things have been chosen for me. But now I want to make my own choice. And you are the person I have chosen.'

She wept after the end of her story and he sat facing her with two things on his mind. The first was that he wanted to strum his guitar and let the strumming accompany her weeping. The second was like a blur in his head: he thought that her story was like placing all the stars in one end of the universe and all the darkness in another and asking the night to choose.

Soon he walked out of the room, while she still wept.

*

When he met Candida at the door to the restaurant, he greeted her casually, though his heart thumped and tumbled with nervousness, expecting that she would forget his name.

'Hello, Higo,' she said.

'You remembered my name.'

She smiled and the dimples easily came. But in her face a troubled existence was written, something that mere dimples could not conceal. He wanted to ask her but he suddenly thought that he was uninvolved.

'You play well.'

'Thanks.'

'It must be fun to you, doing what you can do.'

By this time they had walked inside and sat down, while the restaurant was being prepared for the evening.

'Why do you think I enjoy playing the guitar?'

'Don't you?'

'You did not answer my question.'

'We all enjoy what we do. I mean, when what we do is talent or skill. But unfortunately, that does not mean that we would enjoy life.'

The words sparked something in him, something that did not sound to him like Nigerian or worldly, for that matter. And her person did not strike him like human. She almost seemed out-of-this-world, that moment, talking about enjoying life.

'Are you enjoying your life?'

She looked away and her fingers began to draw an imaginary line on the table they shared. She shook her head suddenly, bent it, and then stood up. That was the second time she walked away from him. But this time he felt sorry that he had thought there was a pomposity in her.

But she came back, as he had come back to Mofe, and said, 'My mother always told me to enjoy my life. That life was fun and simpler than we took it.' She was looking away, at a distance. He followed her eyes, and found that it rested on a black stain on the floor.

'Tell me about your mother.'

'I will tell you about my father and mother. He is South-African. A white South-African. There was the apartheid and it was impossible for a white man to love a black woman. Their wedding was a secret. Everything for them was secret. But it became really dangerous to continue. So they had to separate. I was three at that time and there was the big fighting in Kwazulu Natal where mother lived. Mother came with me to Nigeria, tracing some of her maternal relatives because, funnily enough, her mother is Nigerian, and I can't remember the complex story of how she found herself in South Africa. But our family is scattered. My mother is somewhere here in Lagos. The last I saw of her, she was planning to open a salon. I felt grown up and I had to leave her.'

'You are a true citizen of the world.'

'A complicated ancestry.'

'Nobody owns you.'

They laughed. She said, looking briefly at him, 'I have to go. I have talked too much.'

*

This time Mofe uncovered herself in the middle of the night and lay beside him on the mattress he had stretched on the floor. He had left the bed for her, out of courtesy, knowing it would be unwholesome for him to accept a woman and let her sleep uncomfortably. She had kept talking about her attraction to him, but this time it was her almost naked body beside him on a night without electricity. She lay there almost till morning, until he awoke from a dream of Candida talking about Mozambique and found that succulent flesh was wholly resting on his bare chest.

'Mofe,' was the single word that came from his lips. There was a sudden flush of anger in him. He moved her body furiously away from his and stood up. She woke up at that moment and what he saw was a face that had been deprived of ecstasy. There was silence making a cliff between them. They were both at the edge of that cliff; he was falling and she was pushing.

'Why are you doing this?'

Her silence and pleading eyes.

'I wish I could tell you to leave. I wish this was not Lagos, that

159

there were houses everywhere and you could just leave me alone!'
He walked away, with his shout still loud in the room, still ringing in
her head.

But when she met him outside, where he leaned on an abandoned
Peugeot, her silence and pleading eyes finally got to him and he
could not shout but just looked away.

'Sorry. I'm sorry.'

'It's okay.' At this point she had stood inches away from him, and
the opening morning sky was glamorous and meaningful and
beautiful.

She said, 'Do you often wish Lagos was London?'

'What kind of question is that?'

'It's a question. Answer it.'

'I don't know. I have never thought about it.'

She laughed. 'I was searching for something to say. You were
suddenly silent and I feared you would suddenly remember what I
had done and get angry again.'

'Is that what you think of me? An angry man?'

'Yes, sometimes. You hardly laugh. Sometimes I want to take
what is in your head and throw it away. And replace it with nothing,
except smiling.'

He looked at her with nothing on his face and said, 'I don't know
what to say.'

'What made you like this? Lagos?'

'What kind of question is that?'

'You are an angry person. If you give me the chance I can change
you.'

'Who taught you that?'

'Nobody. I want to change you.'

He laughed. 'Who do you think you are? God?'

Then she looked at herself and found she was only wearing a
negligee and the morning had opened fully. Then she walked back
inside.

*

The following time he saw Candida, she had dull eyes and wore no
make-up. Her beauty was still there, only it had a certain maturity
and plainness about it. Just as if it was a sun shining on a rainy day,
the rain overpowered the sun and the sun was just an insignificant

feature in the sky. When she saw him, she found an empty seat and sat down. Again, the restaurant was being prepared for the evening.

'What is wrong?'

Dull silence, like the rain overpowering the sun.

'Is it someone?'

Her eyes sparked at that one.

'Yes?'

'Yes.'

'Who?'

'I have found a house.'

'All this while…'

'Yes, I lived with him.'

Jealousy sneered at him, and he said 'Why did you leave?' But she replied, 'Do you want to come to my house?' He said yes. There was uneasiness about his response and her voice. Like a tug-of-war of uneasy voices.

'Tell me what is wrong.' She looked away and just like the previous time, she began to draw imaginary lines on the table.

'Please.'

'What?'

'Don't ask. Just leave me as I am.'

'Who are you?'

'Please. Go and forget you knew me.'

'Why?'

'Please.'

He was silent. When he would think about what he said next, he would think that he was a fool, just a fool that spoke nonsense, that he was a lion diving into the water to kill its shadow and, of course, drowned itself. 'I love you.'

But her eyes were not surprised when she looked at him. Her eyes were simply tired, nothing coloured in them, and he was only frustrated that he had said it. She put both her hands on his, briefly, then took them away and stood up. She sat again, found a piece of paper and wrote her address.

When he thought about that moment, he would do so in a haze, her hands resting on his, the warmth from her hands and the warmth passing as quickly as it had come.

It was still a haze when she said, 'My father is coming back for us. He traced my mother and my mother traced me.'

*

Terrifying and disconcerting, she said, was the dream she'd had. The masquerades circled around him while she stood watching, helpless. They struck him with their clubs and other weapons she could not identify until his blood flowed. His blood was not red, but black.

'So what do you want to do?'

'My mother is a prophetess. Let's go and see her.'

'Your mother is a prophetess?'

'Yes. In Cherubim and Seraphim church.'

'Oh,' he laughed.

'I'm serious. I'm concerned about you.'

'It was a dream.'

'You don't believe in dreams?'

'Has Lagos changed because of dreams?'

When she saw that he was insistent, she silently decided to go and see her mother alone.

*

Her gone, he felt suddenly free. He decided to see Candida in her new house, talk to her about his love for her, and maybe get her to love him. While he walked, it was not the unavailability of buses that he thought about. It was not the gutters with green algae, or the raucous voices, or the women retying their wrappers in the open street and showing dirty underwear, or the naked children running around, or the men playing gambling games of draft and checkers. It was about his life, how he was on a par with the people of that street, because Lagos had made all their lives. Lagos determined what one did, the women one loved, the church or mosque one attended. In his life, it was Lagos that had given him a guitar and he played it. It was Lagos that had forced Paulina on him. It was Lagos that had made him inexplicably love Candida, without knowing who she was or what she did. And then, in his final analysis, Lagos was a difficult foe, a maddened force that would not leave until it had it made.

Her house was easy to locate, the last house on the street, a two-storey that had rooms in every part of it, a two-storey that looked as shaky as Paulina's house would have looked before it fell. He could easily decipher that the first floor was the same with the ground floor, a row of rooms left and right, so that, in all, there were about twenty rooms. The piece of paper in his hands said she lived up, her room being the second on the right.

He recognised her crying when he came near. There was stillness in his heart, then hurry, like a lizard nodding before it saw the moth. When he got to the door, he knocked once, then twice, and then he pushed it open.

Her face was in her hands and there was a man standing, holding a belt. It was her, crying, and it was Bollie holding the belt. But Bollie did not face him when he spoke, but her. 'Oh, he is one of them,' and then he raised the belt. Higo held the belt and it did not land on Candida.

'Stay out of this.'

'Why?'

'Do you know her? That she is a prostitute? That she rented this house so that her customers could come easily and I would not disturb them?'

Higo looked at her and she moved her eyes and she began to draw imaginary lines on the bed she was sat on. But he did not care. 'Don't touch her again.'

'Who are you to tell me that?'

'Who are you to beat her?'

'Her boyfriend.'

Higo simply smiled a mocking smile. 'Don't touch her again.' But Bollie raised the belt and it landed on Candida.

*

When Higo thought about what he did to Bollie, later, he would think about *love* and its strange and wicked power of madness. He went to Bollie and struck his face hard enough that it brought blood. Bollie responded with a blow of his own and both men started a fight. Higo easily found a weapon, a stone that was used to wedge the slack door from sliding backwards. The stone ended the fight. It was raised a few inches from Bollie's head and it landed on it and he fell and soon there was enough blood on the floor to discolour a river.

His fall awoke both of them: Candida and Higo. She bent to the fallen man while he stood watching, his hands like an *iroko* crushed by an irredeemable tornado. The fallen man became like a cock

163

struggling between here and there, wanting life but ending up meeting death.

She looked up at him and when he would recall it later, he would think that in her eyes was a mixture of surprise and something else he could not identify. Higo looked back at her, with many things in his head like a thousand cobwebs, and then he walked away.

City of Singers

The shadows imprinted themselves in his heart and they were in the form of a dream, a dream about masquerades, masquerades circling and killing him. The dream was still vivid when he packed his things into a bag and, though he wanted to feel like a man who had killed a man, his head still felt like one with a thousand cobwebs.

'Please. Don't go away.' Mofe was there, all along. She had come from her mother, bearing deadly prophecies of more darkness and more masquerades circling and killing him, of more evil happening to him.

'I am running away. It is not that I want to go. I killed Bollie and I cannot go to prison.'

'There must be a way. Mama said you should not go. Her prophecies always come true.'

'I don't believe in prophecies.'

That moment his strength failed him and he sat on the bed, but he did not cry. It bothered Mofe that he did not cry and that he took the prophecy with levity. The prophecy was clear about the darkness and the masquerades. And the instruction was clear, 'Don't let him leave Lagos.' Yet, she saw his determination, his masculinity overpowering her.

'Please,' she said again.

This time her plea made him stand and end his packing.

'Please. Stay. I would confess I did it. You would be free.'

'Are you crazy?'

'Where are you going to?'

'Anywhere.'

'You see? You have no where. Just stay.'

'I am joining the army. They are recruiting in Kaduna.'

His masculinity shone in its full armour and it did its final overpowering.

But when he was packing his guitar, she suddenly said, 'Play one last time. For me.' He agreed, and he told her, 'Outside.'

It was night and the words of the song and the sound of the guitar seemed to sail above them to the stars, perhaps to create more stars or perhaps to illumine them. They were sitting in front of his room where the restaurant and the night were visible and the darkness not powerful, because the song and the guitar seemed to create more stars and the stars illuminated the darkness.

I returned to the beginning
To find myself there
But instead of me there
I found you and me.

Higo wanted to play more, to let the guitar ring forever. But Mofe was looking elsewhere, at the distance. He stood and touched her hair, ruffled it, and left her to watch the night. Then, he went inside again, returning with his luggage. He met her in the same way and there was just a silent 'oh' when he passed her. Then he walked into the night with his baggage.

Green Beret

Before Higo sang with Mofe, he went to Candida. It was becoming dark then, and when he walked into her room, she was sitting on the bed. Though it was dark enough to require a candle, she had none and so the darkness easily stretched its hoary darkness infinitely into the night.

He said to her, 'I am sorry.' When she had just continued to stare, he said, 'I am going away. I am going to join the army.'

She raised her eyes to him and responded, 'Why are you joining the army?'

'It appears significant for me. My father was a soldier. Maybe I can do more than he did. I want to be like my father. I want to do better than my father.'

'You must go quick. I told the police.'

That shocked him. He was not shocked that she told the police. He was shocked that when she said she told the police her voice became shaky and then she began to sob.

He left her that way and then walked into the full-grown darkness to get his baggage.

It is said that Higo tried to return to Candida on his way to Kaduna, but that when he arrived she was absent and that her door was unlocked. That rattled him, because, when he found a bus, he was still morose and angry over not having been able to tell her he loved her.

It is said that Candida went to her mother the night Higo left and that together they had gone to South Africa to meet her father. But it is also said that Candida returned and that, when she returned, there were letters for her from Higo. The first words of the first letter read: *I joined the Army and next month I would be among those going to Liberia for peacekeeping.* And the last words were: *I always love you.* She decided to read it quickly so that the pain would not return.

In the second letter, his words were brief. *Things are happening very fast here. The rebels know we are taking over and so they have concentrated their efforts in Monrovia alone. We will be going there. These rebels are very dangerous and I think that we will have to be careful as we go.*

It is said that someone confessed to the crime of killing Bollie, but that, when he was taken to court, no evidence was found and the whole killing was questioned and the person was acquitted. By then, Bollie had been buried. When Candida heard this, she started re-reading Higo's letters until the paper was creased and the handwriting crumpled and illegible.

It is said that Candida mourned about his death in Lagos. She had waited for more of his letters but received none. Then, one night, the night she believed he had died, she believed that, when the gun aimed at his chest rang, she felt a pain in her own chest. When this happened, she stood up from her bed, where she had been holding his last letter against the candlelight, and opened the window. She saw him in the night, a night she thought very dark, walking away, and she finally thought that the night itself had swallowed him.

But if all of this had not happened, Higo would still be in his mother's room, fondling the green beret left by his father and waiting for sunset so that he could carry his guitar to the frontage and play. That way he would never have met Candida, never have killed Bollie, never have gone to Liberia or never even have died.

If only all of this had not happened.

Notes on the Contributors

Abubakar Adam Ibrahim holds a degree in Mass Communication from the University of Jos, Jos, Nigeria. He has written for *Vanguard* newspaper, one of Nigeria's foremost newspapers, and his short fictions have been published locally and internationally. In 2007, he won the BBC African Performance Playwriting Competition and his first novel, *The Quest for Nina,* was released by Raider Publishing International, New York, United States. He has recently finished work on his second novel.

Ikeogu Oke was born at Akanu Ohafia, in south-eastern Nigeria, in 1967, and educated at the University of Calabar and at the University of Nigeria, where he earned a BA in English and Literary Studies and an MA in Literature, respectively. Since 1988, his poems have been published in various magazines, journals and other forms of periodicals in his country, Nigeria, and in the United States, including *Unity Magazine* (published by the Unity School of Christianity, Kansas City, Missouri), *DISCOVERY* (published in Braille by the John Milton Society for the Blind, New York), and *FARAFINA* (published by Kachifo Limited, Lagos). He has also published a collection of poems, *Where I Was Born* (2002, revised 2003), and his articles have appeared widely in reputed Nigerian newspapers, including *The Guardian, This Day, Vanguard, Champion, The Sun,* the *Nigerian Tribune,* and in the London-based *News Africa* magazine. He recently started trying his hand at writing prose fiction, having just completed a book-length, epic poem, *The Heresiad* (in rhymed 'lyrical pentameters' and with great potentials for orchestration), which is currently seeking a publisher. He is currently a Standards Editor at Timbuktu Media, Lagos, publishers of NEXT newspaper.

Peter Ike Amadi was born in Enugu town, Nigeria to Igbo parents Chief Dr A.O Amadi, formally a lecturer of the University of Nigeria, Nsukka and Cecilia Amadi, a business woman. He grew up with three other siblings Uchenna, Ngozi and Chinyere whilst living at the University of Nigeria, Nsukka after spending four years in Swansea, Wales. He studied at the same university graduating with a B.Sc in Geography. He worked for four years as an assistant manager at a popular cinema in Lagos, Nigeria and is presently a staff writer for an entertainment magazine also in Lagos. He is highly interested in writing mystery/suspense stories and his literary influences are wide and diverse ranging from Agatha Christie, John Connolly and Arthur C. Clark to Nigerian writers like Kalu Okpi, Cyprian Ekwensi and Chinua Achebe. Also his writing has been influenced by movies, TV series and comic books. He hopes to write stories that are ambitious, morally complex, insightful but most importantly highly entertaining.

Jumoke Verissimo writes poetry and short stories. She works as a copywriter, and also as a freelance journalist for newspapers and several magazines. Many of her poems and short stories have appeared in several anthologies and magazines. She is the author of *I Am Memory,* a collection of poems, which she has read/performed in different venues in Nigeria. Jumoke was born in Lagos, Nigeria and continues to live there. She is working on her next book.

Ifeanyi Ogboh was born in Lagos, Nigeria in 1980. Though a doctoral candidate of the Chemical Engineering Department of the University of Lagos, he enjoys writing short stories depicting life in Nigeria. He has been writing short stories for online magazines since 2004. He also enjoys soccer, scrabble, travelling and reading novels. He lives and works in Lagos, Nigeria.

Rotimi (Timi) Ogunjobi is editor and publisher of *The Redbridge Review* (www.redbridgereview.co.uk) and *The Lagos Literary and Arts Journal* (**www.lagosliterary journal.com**). His writings have featured in several publications and writing projects worldwide and his short story 'Brain Surgery on the Highway', which was first published in 2002 by Queens Quarterly - of Queens University, Canada, has also been featured as study material in some Business Management and Marketing courses. Another short story has previously won runners-up prize in an Association of Nigerian Authors organized competition. Rotimi Ogunjobi attended Government College Ibadan and later University of Lagos where he obtained a degree in Civil Engineering. He has afterwards worked in several engineering, construction and IT companies in Nigeria and UK. He is presently a freelance Software and Technical Communication Consultant. Rotimi Ogunjobi has numerous other writing credits.

Uchechukwu Peter Umezurike, popularly known as 'Uche Peter Umez', is the author of the award-winning *Sam and the Wallet* [children's novella], *Dark through the Delta* (poems), *Aridity of Feelings* (poems), and *Tears in Her Eyes* (short stories). His collection of children's stories, *Tim the Monkey and Other Stories,* is forthcoming from African First Publishers. His awards include: winner, *2008 BSU Creative Writing competition*; Highly Commended winner, *Commonwealth Short Story Competition*, 2006 and 2008 respectively; winner, *ANA/Funtime Prize for Children's Fiction,* 2006 and 2008 respectively; finalist/runner-up both for the *2007 Nigerian LNG Prize for Literature*, and the *2007 ANA/Lantern Prize for Children's Literature*. An Alumnus of the *International Writing Program* (IWP), USA, Caine Prize for African Writing Workshop, his short fiction, poems, reviews and non-fiction have been published on-line and in print. He is one of the selected participants for the 2009 UNESCO-Aschberg Bursary.

Tolu Ogunlesi was born in 1982. He is the author of a collection of poetry, *Listen to the geckos singing from a balcony* (Bewrite Books, 2004), and of a novella, *Conquest and Conviviality* (Hodder Murray, 2008). His fiction and poetry have appeared in *Wasafiri, Farafina, Sable, The London Magazine, Nano2ales, Orbis, Magma* and the *PEN Anthology of New Nigerian Writing,* and in translation in *Verdensmagasinet X, Karogs* and *Buran.* In 2007, he won a Dorothy Sargent Rosenberg poetry prize, and in 2009 was shortlisted for the inaugural PEN/Studzinski Literary Prize. He has been a guest writer at the Nordic Africa Institute, Uppsala, Sweden (2008) and the Center of West African Studies, University of Birmingham, England (2009). He currently works as a freelance writer and editor in Lagos, Nigeria.

Soji Cole graduated from the Department of Theatre Arts, University of Ibadan in Nigeria.

Alpha Emeka is the author of the novel, *The Carnival* (Cehmes Publications, 2007). He is a native of Lokpanta in Abia State, Nigeria. He graduated from St. Murumba College, Jos, and is currently a student of Building at the University of Jos. *Aunty Florence,* his second novel, was published in 2008. He has won a number of literary awards which include: an essay competition organised by the Ministry of Education Plateau State and as first runner up, Mathew Mzega Price for short stories. His short stories have also been selected for the British Council's Radiophonics project. He is the Vice President of 'Dreams Literary and Arts' and a member of the Association of Nigerian Authors (ANA). He lives in Jos, the Plateau State Capital.

Emmanuel Iduma was born in 1989. His stories and poems have been published both online and print. He was a finalist of the 1st Word in Action Literary Contest 2008, and a winner of the Avant Garde Poetry Contest 2008. Currently, he is an undergraduate student of Law at Obafemi Awolowo University, Ile-Ife, where he resides and freelances on several news agencies. He also blogs weekly on www.edumablog.blogspot.com. Recently, he started an electronic magazine with a friend, and it has been received with critical acclaim in the Nigerian literary community. The electronic magazine can be found on www.sarabamag.com. He is working on a novel and a story collection.

About the Editor

Emma Dawson currently lectures at Keele University. She works at the intersection of postcolonial writing, pedagogy and the emergent field of World Englishes literature. She has published a number of academic articles in the field, and her Ph.D addressed the teaching of World Englishes literature in schools in England. As a result of her studies, she published *Read Around*, a ground-breaking series for secondary schools (CCC Press, 2008). She is the general Editor of CCCP's World Englishes Literature imprint, and in its fiction series is currently editing anthologies of short stories from Uganda, Kenya, Singapore and Malaysia (forthcoming, 2010/11). *'The Spirit Machine' and other new short stories from Cameroon* was published in June 2009 and is the first in the collection of anthologies of the World Englishes Fiction series.

www.ingramcontent.com/pod-product-compliance
Lightning Source LLC
Chambersburg PA
CBHW032031050726
47590CB00006B/2374